Herbert Henry Hudson

The Malay Orthography

Herbert Henry Hudson

The Malay Orthography

ISBN/EAN: 9783337288556

Printed in Europe, USA, Canada, Australia, Japan

Cover: Foto ©Andreas Hilbeck / pixelio.de

More available books at **www.hansebooks.com**

قد مڤتاكن

تليسن بهاس ملايو.

مرتب

علمو هبوڠن حروف دان رڠکاين حروف ڤرکتأن

THE MALAY ORTHOGRAPHY

BY

HERBERT HENRY HUDSON

(Deputy Registrar, Supreme Court, Singapore, Straits Settlements)

SINGAPORE

KELLY & WALSH, LIMITED

1892

TO HIS EXCELLENCY

Sir CECIL CLEMENTI SMITH,

KNIGHT GRAND CROSS OF THE MOST DISTINGUISHED ORDER OF ST. MICHAEL AND ST. GEORGE,
GOVERNOR OF THE STRAITS SETTLEMENTS,

These Pages

ARE, BY PERMISSION, MOST RESPECTFULLY

DEDICATED BY

THE AUTHOR.

CONTENTS.

ERRATA.

Page 25, 15th and 16th lines,—

For   The Malays call it تا ڤنجغ *ta panjang* or "long
   t", and often use it incorrectly in place of the
   ordinary ت *t*.

Read   The Malays call it تا بندر *ta bundar* and often use
   it incorrectly for the ordinary ت or تا ڤنجغ
   ta panjang.

Page 45, 18th line,—

For   مغلبر
Read   مغلمبر

INTRODUCTORY PREFACE.

THE following pages consist of the amplification of certain notes made in studying the Malay Orthography. The subject being one the principles of which are little understood by most of the persons whose services are available as teachers, great difficulty is commonly experienced by the student in getting from them any reliable information. The spelling in the better known Malay compositions is by no means consistent throughout. There is a native pamphlet dealing with the subject, but it is of little value. The works of European authors meet with more approval, but these are nearly all out of print, and difficult of access. Probably every student of Malay experiences the same difficulty in obtaining instruction on this subject, for it must be remembered that the services of the more highly educated Malays are rarely available for this purpose. The general principles could be explained in a few oral lessons, if a competent teacher could be met with, but it is the difficulty of finding persons capable of imparting this knowledge, which has induced the offer of this work to the student. There are a number of moot points which must be left for the ultimate decision of the Malays themselves, but by far the larger part of the subject is common ground, and of extreme simplicity. Each writer on this subject has freely used the works of his predecessors, and a very considerable part of the text of this book consists of extracts and quotations, mainly taken from the works hereunder mentioned, but, from the necessity of rendering the text consecutive and concordant, the wording has been often changed and adapted

The extracts from the Abbé FAVRE'S book, which has been largely used, though not uniformly followed, have been freely translated, and often intermixed with quotations from other authors, and new matter, and the equivalents in Roman letters of the Malay words and sounds in his book, being written for French readers, are here differently rendered, for, it was thought advisable, in order to avoid complication, to adapt all such to the plan of this work. It was found, that to attempt to mark each quotation, or extract, as such, would render a very large number of notes and explanations necessary, and seriously cramp and confine the text. The author, therefore, humbly apologizes for the liberties he has taken, and testifies his sincere admiration for the learning, skill and labour which have produced the works in question, and, in answer to a charge of plagiarism which might be made, freely and fully admits that, but for them, these pages would never have been written.

The whole has been frequently revised and re-written, and carefully compared with every work dealing with the subject, to which access could be obtained. The text has been divided into sections and paragraphs for the sake of making some break, and for convenience of reference, but the various parts are at times so nearly connected, that this arrangement is not in all respects satisfactory. The fact that this subdivision leads to a certain amount of repetition, is not perhaps a great disadvantage in a work of this kind.

The transliteration of the Arabic characters in Malay words has been rendered in italics, and the translation placed between inverted commas. The latter has been made as literal as possible, even at the expense of the English, in order to increase the general utility of the work.

The mixture of the different kinds of type has created considerable difficulty in the setting up, especially because great varieties of founts are not available here, and the indulgence of the reader is requested for all deficiencies. Two defects are very apparent—first, in consequence of the large bodies of the Arabic type the vowel signs appear at too great a distance from the letters they accompany ; and secondly, the type used does not admit of the insertion of a *hamzah* between two joined letters except by employing with it that which appears like a substantive letter (ﺍ) . The sincere thanks of the author are due to Mr. H. L. NORONHA of the Government Printing Office for his kind assistance in seeing these pages through the press.

H. H. H.

Singapore, January, 1892.

EUROPEAN WORKS QUOTED.

A Grammar of the Malay Language, by WILLIAM MARSDEN, F. R. S. London, 1812.

An Attempt to elucidate the Principles of Malayan Orthography, by W. ROBINSON. Fort Marlborough, 1823.

A Grammar and Dictionary of the Malay Language, by JOHN CRAWFURD, F. R. S. London, 1852.

Grammaire de la langue malaise, par l'Abbé P. FAVRE. Vienne, 1876.

THE MALAY ORTHOGRAPHY

SECTION I.

GENERAL.

1. THE subject of which this work treats is not free from difficulty, not on account of any great complexity, but because of its uncertainty, the Malays themselves having in the main neglected to regulate it by rule and principle, and they, for the most part, at the present day, allow themselves a very considerable license in the spelling of words.

2. When the Arabic orthography was first applied to Malay, it was taken as a whole, with its elaborate and cumbersome diacritical points, vowel signs, and orthographical marks accompanying the letters, and it was used, so far as seemed requisite, to reproduce the Malay sounds. A large part of it was quite unnecessary, but no attempt appears to have ever been made to formulate and define a modification of it. The addition of six letters, to meet the sounds for which the Arabic had no corresponding letters, was the most important change. At the present day, however, it may be said that the vowel signs are never used in ordinary writing, and that two only of the orthographical marks are ever applied to native words, but to account for the traditional spelling of

many words, the presence of some of them must be supposed, and without a knowledge of the principles of their application, nothing like correctness in writing Malay can well be attained.

3. The omission of the vowel signs, and an imperfect knowledge of the use of the other marks, have led to a much freer use of those letters called weak letters, which, in one of their uses, partake of the character of vowels, and it is probable that a charge may be made, that the application of the principles laid down in these pages will result in the spelling of some Malay words in a manner inconsistent with the more general practice of the Malays themselves. If the practice of spelling certain words, in a manner at variance with those principles, were universal, or if there were any recognized authority for such spelling accepted by the Malays in general, or, if the practice were reducible to, or explainable by, any rule or principle, then such a charge would be unanswerable. Not only is the contrary of all three the case, but it is believed that if the principles, with which it is proposed to deal, be carefully considered, their application will in no case lead to the spelling of a word in a manner inconsistent with the practice of one or other of the better known Malay writers and for which good authority cannot be found. But the spelling in all native writings varies considerably, and there is no accepted authority to decide which is correct. In those cases in which a conventional spelling seems to have met with anything like general acceptation, it has been carefully noted.

SECTION II.

THE USE OF THE ABABIC LETTERS.

4. Whatever may have been the original characters employed in Malay Orthography (if any native Alphabet ever
existed*), it has, for centuries past, been exclusively written
upon the Arabic system, and without some knowledge of that
system, it would be impossible to arrive at anything like a
thorough knowledge of the language, but it is a system foreign
to Malay, and, as commonly written, viz., without the vowel
signs, insufficient to convey the pronunciation of the words.
That these could be rendered by the Roman letters with
more precision and clearness than by the Arabic, has the
support of FAVRE, but although the Dutch have reduced the
writing of Malay in Roman letters to some sort of system,
yet the Dutch spelling is misleading to an English reader, and
no rendering in Roman letters has been generally accepted.

5. The combined Alphabet, i. e., the Arabic with the six
additions, consists of 34 letters : of these, one (ڠ) is now
never used, 19 are sufficient for the primitive Malay, and 13
are only found in words of foreign origin. One letter (ݢ)
is used in primitive Malay words as a substitute for another
(ک) , when final, but, when used in foreign words, has a
different value assigned to it. It, therefore, finds a place in
both lists, making the total of the one 20, and that of the
latter 14.

6. Of these 14 letters, the sounds are foreign to the

* It is supposed that the Korinchi characters were once used.

Malays, and a very wide divergence in their pronunciation
will be met with, but the Arabs, or those who who have
acquired a knowledge of Arabic, are the religious, and for the
most part also the secular, instructors. Verses from the
Korān are taught and expounded in the schools, the prayers
are in Arabic, and, though as little understood by the majority
as the Latin prayers were in ancient days by the peasantry in
England, yet some knowledge of the sounds is acquired, and
those who study Arabic delight in displaying their knowledge,
either by giving to the Arabic words adopted into Malay their
original pronunciation and orthography, or by employing in a
somewhat pedantic manner Arabic words, in some instances,
notwithstanding that the native Malay words are competent
to convey the meaning required. The result is that the
Malay may be said to be tinged with Arabic, and the native
writers freely use words from the latter language to convey a
meaning not readily expressed in their own tongue. The
Arabic has, however, had no effect upon the grammatical construction of Malay, it has enriched it with a number of words,
and has supplied the system of Orthography, but beyond this
its influence does not extend. There are indications leading
to the supposition that the employment of the Arabic system
of orthography in an imperfect form, may have had some
effect upon the pronunciation, and caused uncertainty as to
the proper vowel sounds in many words.

7. Nearly all the words adopted from foreign languages
other than Arabic, for instance, Sanscrit, Persian, Indian,
Chinese, European, and the numerous languages of the

Archipelago, of which it is said that only the Javanese and
Malay are derived from a common stock, have been reduced to
the Malay standard, and brought within the compass of the 20
letters above-mentioned—a natural and proper process, for
words are adopted for utility, and to enrich, not to complicate
or debase, a language. To this process some of the
adopted Arabic words have already been subjected, though
the greater number preserve their orthography, but the operation has been retarded with regard to the remainder by the
intimate association of the Arabic language with the Muhammadan religion, which is that of the Malays, tending to keep
up a certain connection between them and the Arabic language, a connection which is further fostered by the venera-
tion which the Malays have towards the race from which
their religion has been drawn, and by the employment of the
same system of orthography in both languages. The latter
statement is made as the result of enquiry as to whether any
native work on the Malay grammar had ever been written.
The invariable answer obtained was :—"We have no grammar
but the Arabic," showing that, as regards their own language,
Malays have little conception of grammar beyond that part
of it called Orthography, for the remainder of the Arabic
Grammar can have absolutely no application to Malay, and
that they consider their Orthography should be regulated by
the Arabic rules.

SECTION III.

THE RADICAL OR PRIMITIVE WORDS.

8. The radical words in Malay are for the most part dis-syllables, with a slight stress or accent on the first, or rather the penultimate syllable. When isolated, the radical word only indicates a general idea, and can rarely be assigned to any particular 'part of speech'. In this state it contains no definition, whether of mood, tense, number, gender, or case. In the course of these pages the word 'radical' will be found frequently used, but it is inaccurate, and is employed only for want of a better term. The Malay language knows no system whatever corresponding to the root and its derivatives in Arabic, and in order, therefore, to avoid misconception, it will be better to define exactly the sense in which the word is here used. 'Radical' is employed to designate both indigenous and adopted words, in their simple form, notwithstanding that such words may have undergone transformation, whether in the language from which they are drawn, or in the Malay itself, provided that they are not accompanied by prefixed or suffixed particles, and have undergone none of the modifications to which, in their derivative forms, they are subject. This definition is taken from FAVRE'S Grammar, and is slightly enlarged from that given by MARSDEN.

SECTION IV.

THE MALAY WORDS IN ROMAN LETTERS.

9. In giving the equivalent of the Arabic characters, the following values have been assigned to the Roman letters :—

*Vowels.**

a = the Italian ' a ' or the sound of ' a ' in ' cart, alms, ah ! '

'(an inverted comma) = the unaccented ' e ' in French as in *de ce que je ne me rappelais pas*, or nearly the sound of ' u ' in ' turn ', ' i ' in ' bird, third, ' the ' e ' in ' aver, vertical.' (*See* par. 49 as to the *inherent vowel*.)

i = the ' e ' in English as in ' be, queen, Eton.' When occurring in a syllable closed by a nasal letter, its sound is modified nearly to that of ' i ' in ' tin, sing, minim.'

e = the ' a ' in English as in ' arid, cane.' When occurring in a syllable closed by nasal letter, its sound is modified nearly to that of ' e ' in ' ten, end, hem.'

u = the double ' o ' in English as in ' boon, room.' (Never the sound of ' u ' in ' use.')

o = the ' o ' in English as in ' only, bone.'

*Diphthongs.**

ay = a combination of ' a ' and ' i ' (a-ee) nearly the sound of ' aye ', or of ' i ' in ' fine, island,' but longer ; the sound of ' ay ' in ' pay ' is often heard, but seems less correct.

aw = a combination of ' a ' and ' u ' (a-oo) nearly the vowel sound in ' cow, allow,' but longer.

---

* The attention of the reader is especially directed to the values to be assigned to the *vowels* and *diphthongs* in the transliteration.

Consonants.

b, d, f = the same letters in English.

g = the hard 'g' as in 'begin, gone, agog.' (Never soft as in 'genius, congeal.')

h = 'h' but an aspirate so soft as in most cases to be hardly perceptible.

ḥ = a very strong aspirate.

j, k = the same letters in English.

ḳ = 'k' in English, but a stronger guttural.

l, m, n = the same letters in English.

ñ = the combined sound of 'ni' in 'senior' or the 'gn' in the French *seigneur, agneau*, the Spanish 'ñ' in *señor*, or the English 'n' in 'news, nuisance.'

p = the same letter in English.

r = as in English, but the Malays mostly give a softer sound to this letter than we do.

s = 's' or 'ss' in English as in 'sincere, custom, toss.' (Never as in 'busy, bosom, or sugar.')

t = 't' in English.

ṭ = 'tt' in English, stronger than 't'.

w, y = as in English (where not employed as vowels).

z = 'z' as in 'lazy' or the 's' in 'busy, refusal.'

The following represent single Arabic letters :—

ths = a sound partaking of 'th' and 's,' a sibilant or whistling sound.

ch = as in 'church.'

kh = a very strong guttural like the 'ch' in the Scotch 'loch' or in the German *Ich*.

sh = as in ' shine, rushing, crash. '

dl = as in ' saddle.'

tl = as in ' cattle.'

gh or ghr = a very strong guttural.

ng = as in ' hanging. ' (The reader is cautioned against se-
parating the components of this sound, or giving to the ' g ' the
sound of ' j ' as in ' changed,' and also against giving it the
sound of a double ' g ' as in ' angle. ') In Malay this sound
may be initial either in a word or syllable.

dz = as in ' adze.'

From this point, therefore, the reader will assign to these
letters, when representing a Malay sound, the values above
given.

10.   In addition to the above, a grave accent (`) has been
employed to mark the presence of the letter called *ain*, and
consonants representing a combined sound have been under-
lined where there is any risk of their being understood to
represent distinct sounds, or if representing separate letters,
have been divided by a point, where there is danger of their
being taken to represent a combined sound. The rendering
in Roman letters of the Malay words is based upon a certain
plan of analysis for the purposes only of this work, viz., the
explanation of the principles of Malay Orthography, and is
not intended as a new method of writing the Malay in Roman letters, nor is it intended to be imitated for the latter
purpose.

11.   The pronunciation of any language should always be
acquired from the lips of a native, and the values here

given are approximate only. The student will find
much assistance in learning the pronunciation of Malay,
if he will habitually consider each consonant, or sound
represented by a combination of consonants in the transliteration,
as primarily unaccompanied by any strongly marked vowel
sound, only adding the latter as circumstances require, thus
b, t, m, p, ch, and *sh,* will be considered as ' *b,* ' *t,* ' *m,* ' *p,*
' *ch,* and ' *sh,* and not *ba, ta, ma, pa, cha* and *sha.* (*See* par. 49
as to the inherent vowel.) This is indeed nothing more than
the modern method of elementary instruction adopted in most
European languages. Thus ' *b + a = ba,* ' *b + o = bo,* and so
on. The special applicability of this to languages written in
the Arabic characters will be seen later.

SECTION V.

PRONUNCIATION.

12. The Malay language, called by them *b'ha-sa m'la-yu* or *b'ha-sa ja-wi*, is singularly free from any difficulty of pronunciation to a European. Its sounds are soft, pleasant and clear to the ear, there is a constant regularity in the relative employment of consonant and vowel, and, as has been observed by MARSDEN, " the attention indeed to smoothness of utterance is " so great that not only in the formation of derivatives are " letters systematically changed in order to please the ear, but "also in words borrowed from Continental tongues the Malays " are accustomed to polish down the rougher consonants to the " standard of their own organs." There is hardly a sound in it which the least practised ear cannot distinguish at the first hearing, and which the least pliable tongue cannot articulate as well at the first attempt as a person practised in the language. For politeness and softness the Malay merits the description applied to it of " The Italian of the East."

13. As follows almost of necessity from the area over which the use of the language extends, numerous variations both in pronunciation and the use of words occur, notable among them are the tendencies in some places to give to vowels in final syllables the sound ' as *ga-s'* for *ga-sak*, *ka-t'* for *ka-ta* (in the latter instance probably correctly as noticed below), and in others the sound of *o* as *ka-to* for *ka-ta*, *b'sor* for *b'sar*, and to pronounce words ending in *k*, as for instance *bayk* 'good,' in some places *bay*, and in others to sound the *k* as broadly as in the English 'spike, dyke.'

14. The written language is, however, fairly regular as has been remarked by MARSDEN, but the oral tongue, both in respect to pronunciation and the use of peculiar personal pronouns and other words, differs considerably. He gives a considerable list of the principal distinctions of dialect at pages 112 *et seq.* of his Grammar, but the subject is one outside the scope of this work.

SECTION VI.

ACCENT.

15. The accent in Malay is very weak, and may be said to consist merely of a prolongation of the vowel sound in one syllable. The great tendency is to place the accent on the penultimate, or last syllable but one, of the word, and when we speak of the accent being moved by the addition of a suffixed particle, it must be clearly borne in mind that the original penultimate (*i. e.*, before the addition of the particle) loses only so much of its length of sound, as naturally follows from the change of the following syllable from a short to a long sound.

16. For these reasons it has been considered, that the division of the syllables of the radical in the Romanized Malay, at the point where the long vowel (if any) occurs, sufficiently conveys to the reader where the accent will be found, and except in a few instances, where the accent does not follow the ordinary course, no sign has been employed to mark it. Where such is the case, the sign used is an acute accent (′), or in some Arabic words the long vowel has been marked as in *ikhlās*. We may add that the accent is very rarely found on the syllable, if open, where the indefinite vowel sound represented by ‘ occurs, as in *p'das* ‘ pungent,' *b'sar* ‘ large,' *k'nal* ‘ to recognize, know, ' but that this forms almost the only exception to the accent being on the penultimate in native bisyllabic radical words.

SECTION VII.

THE ALPHABET.

17. The following Table gives the full Arabic-Malay Alphabet :—

Letter	Power	Name	Letter	Power	Name
ا	a	الف *alif*	ط	t	طا *ta*
ب	b	با *ba*	ظ	tl	ظا *tla*
ت	t	تا *ta*	ع		عين *ain*
ث	ths	ثا *thsa*	غ	gh	غين *ghain*
ج	j	جيم *jim*	ڠ	ng	ڠا *nga*
چ	ch	چا *cha*	ف	f	فا *fa*
ح	h	حا *ha*	ڤ	p	ڤا *pa*
خ	kh	خا *kha*	ق	k	قڤ *kap*
د	d	دال *dal*	ك	k	كاڤ *kap*
ذ	dz	ذال *dzal*	ݢ	g	ݢا *ga*
ڎ	d	دا *da*	ل	l	لم *lam*
ر	r	را *ra*	م	m	ميم *mim*
ز	z	زا *za* or زي *zi*	ن	n	نون *nun*
س	s	سيم *sim*	و	w, u, o.	واو *waw*
ش	sh	شيم *shim*	ه	h	ها *ha*
ص	s	صاد *sad*	ي	y, i, e.	يا *ya*
ض	dl	ضاد *dlad*	ں	ñ	ڽ *ña*

To which are sometimes superfluously added ء همزة *hamzah*, and لا *la*, لم الف *lam alif*.

18. Of the full Alphabet the following six are the additions made to the Arabic Alphabet :—

   ڽ *ña*   ڬ *ga*   ڤ *pa*   ڠ *nga*   ڎ *da**   چ *cha*

which, it will be bbserved, have been formed from certain Arabic letters, by the simple expedient of increasing to three the number of the diacritical points.

19. It has been already remarked that certain of the Arabic letters are unnecessary to the primitive Malay, and occur only in words of foreign origin. Subjoined is a list of each, as well as tables showing the forms which the letters take according to their position in a word, and their relation to the other letters thereof.

20. The natural alphabet of the language as formulated by FAVRE is given, followed by his table showing how the sounds required in the primitive Malay correspond to 19 letters of the Alphabet. The utility of this classification will be seen later.

---

* It is difficult to settle at the present day why the character ڎ *da* was formed, though it must have been to meet some sound foreign to Arab ears. There is a peculiar soft sound sometimes heard from Malay lips nearly corresponding to ட in Tamil, but difficult of pronunciation by Europeans; it approaches the sound of '*dr*'. At the present day this sound is represented by ر *r*, but it is quite possible that it may have been intended by the Arabs to be represented by د while the simple '*d*' as in the English sound was to be represented by ڎ. CRAWFURD makes the following comment :—"The first '*d*' (د) in the Malay Alphabet is a dental and corresponds with the Arabic dental of the same class. In English pronunciation it is found only when '*d*' is followed by '*r*' and coalesces with it. The second '*d*' (ڎ) * * * is a palatal, sometimes called a cerebral, and corresponds with the European letter." We have never met with the character ڎ in Malay writing. "This letter never occurs." (ROBINSON). "Always found in the Alphabets written by the Malays for elementary instruction, but rarely if ever occurs in their books" (MARSDEN).

[16]

TABLE II.
TWENTY LETTERS USED IN NATIVE MALAY WORDS.

Letter	Power	Name		Letter	Power	Name	
ا	a	الف	alif	* ق	k	قاف	kap
ب	b	با	ba	ك	k	كاف	kap
ت	t	تا	ta	ك	g	گا	ga
ج	j	جيم	jim	ل	l	لام	lam
چ	ch	چا	cha	م	m	ميم	mim
د	d	دال	dal	ن	n	نون	nun
ر	r	را	ra	و	w,u,o.	واو	waw
س	s	سيم	sim	ه	h	ها	ha
غ	ng	غا	nga	ي	y,i,e.	يا	ya
ف	p	فا	pa	ث	ñ	پا	ña

TABLE III.
FOURTEEN LETTERS USED IN WORDS OF FOREIGN ORIGIN.

Letter	Power	Name		Letter	Power	Name	
ث	ths	ثا	thsa	ض	dl	ضاد	dlad
ح	h	حا	ha	ط	t	طا	ta
خ	kh	خا	kha	ظ	tl	ظا	tla
ذ	dz	ذال	dzal	ع		عين	ain
ز	z	زا	za	غ	gh	عين	ghain
ش	sh	شيم	shim	ف	f	فا	fa
ص	s	صاد	sad	ق	k	قاف	kap

* The Malays generally employ ی instead of ك when final in a word, but without meaning thereby to indicate the more guttural sound of the former letter, which it has in words of foreign origin. The sound of *k*, medial in a word, but at the end of a syllable, is rendered by ق in words coming from the Sanscrit; as لقس *laksa* '10,000' (in Hind. 100,000), لقسن *laksa-na* 'like,' وقسين *paksi-na* 'the north, the left,' دقسين *daksi-na* 'the south, the right,' وقس *paksa* 'force,' &c. This letter therefore finds a place in both tables.

TABLE IV.

FORMS OF THE LETTERS.

Isolated	Final	Medial	Initial	Isolated	Final	Medial	Initial
ا	ا	ل	ا	ق	ق	ﻘ	ﻗ
ب	ب	ﺒ	ﺑ	ك	ك	ﻜ	ﻛ
ت	ت	ﺘ	ﺗ	ك	ك	ﻜ	ﻛ
ج	ج	ﺠ	ﺟ	ل	ل	ﻠ	ﻟ
ج	ج	ﺠ	ﺟ	م	م	ﻤ	ﻣ
د	د	ﺪ	د	ن	ن	ﻨ	ﻧ
ر	ر	ﺮ	ر	و	و	ﻮ	و
س	س	ﺴ	ﺳ	ه	ه	ﻬ	ﻫ
غ	غ	ﻐ	ﻏ	ي	ي	ﻴ	ﻳ
ف	ف	ﻔ	ﻓ	ث	ث	ﺜ	ﺗ
ث	ث	ﺜ	ﺗ	ض	ض	ﻀ	ﺿ
ح	ح	ﺤ	ﺣ	ط	ط	ﻄ	ﻃ
خ	خ	ﺨ	ﺧ	ظ	ظ	ﻈ	ﻇ
ذ	ذ	ﺬ	ذ	ع	ع	ﻌ	ﻋ
ز	ز	ﺰ	ز	غ	غ	ﻐ	ﻏ
ش	ش	ﺸ	ﺷ	ف	ف	ﻔ	ﻓ
ص	ص	ﺼ	ﺻ	ق	ق	ﻘ	ﻗ

TABLE V.
FORMS OF THE LETTERS IN COMBINATION.

Letter	Isolated	Final	Medial	Initial
ا	واﻩ	دنيا	جاوﻩ بهاس	اڤي ايٖر
ب	جواب	سبب	سبب ممباو	بات بهارو
ت	برت	ساكت	بتاڤ	تاڤق
ج	راج	بلنج	منجادي	جنتن
چ	باچ	ڤنچ	كچل	چهاري
د	داد	ڤد	بندڠ	درين
ر	بار	دبر	بري	رمڤس
س	بهاس	اتس	بسر	سمڤي
غ	اورڠ	يغ	سڠكه	غري
ف	اف	اتڤ	تڤي	فاتت
ق	چردق	انق	لقسان	قدرﺓ
ك	بوك	ملك	بكس	كاسه كورڠ
ڬ	سورٮٚ	تٮٚٮٚ	بهاڬي	ڬاجه ڬويڠ
ل	اول	كڤل	بيلغ	لنتس
م	كم	انم	سمنتار	منٚغ
ن	ورن	اكن	كنل	نايق نينڠ
و	بورو	برتمو	بوت	واج
ه	جاوﻩ	روﻣﻪ	بهاس بهارو	هاري
ي	اي	تڠٚكي هاري تڤي	تياد	يادٝت
ى	تان	استرين	لنڤ	ڤات

TABLE VI.
FORMS OF THE LETTERS IN COMBINATION.

Letter	Isolated	Final	Medial	Initial
ث	ثلاث	حديث	مثل	ثابت
ح	روح	صح	صحبت	حكم
خ	شرخ	شيخ	تخت	خيمة
ذ	اذان	هومذ	لذة	ذكر
ز	دوز	عز	عزة	زمان
ش	عرش	تشويش	مانشي	شه‌دن
ص	اخلاص	حلص	فصل	صبر
ض	عروض	حايض	حضرة	ضرورة
ط	سرط	واسط	شيطان	طمع
ظ	محفوظ	لفظ	عظمة	ظاهر
ع	جماع	طمع	ضعيف	عالم
غ	بلوغ	بالغ	مشغل	غاين
ف	عرف	صف	صفة	فكر
ق	صادق	حق	تقدير	قدرة

TABLE VII.

The Natural Alphabet of the Malay language as formulated by the Abbé FAVRE :—

Vowels (6).

a   '   i   e   u   o

Aspirate (1).

h

Semi-vowels (2).

y   w

Consonants (15).

GUTTURALS ...	k	... ...	...	hard.
	g	... ...	...	soft.
	ng	...	...	nasal.
PALATALS ...	ch	... ...	...	hard.
	j	...	...	soft.
	ñ	... ...	...	nasal.
DENTALS ...	t	... ...	...	hard
	d	... ...	...	soft.
	n	... ...	...	nasal.
LABIALS ...	p	... ...	...	hard.
	b	... ...	...	soft.
	m	... ...	...	nasal.
LIQUIDS ...	r			
	l			
SIBILANT	s			

NOTE.—This classification may be questioned, and is at variance with those both of CRAWFURD and ROBINSON, but it forms an easy means of committing to memory certain changes caused by prefixed particles.

TABLE VIII,

Showing how the Natural Alphabet corresponds with the Arabic-Malay Alphabet (the foreign elements as shown in Table III being omitted).

Class	Nature	Form of the Letter				Name		Power
		Isola-ted	Final	Medial	Initial			
Weak letters, semi-vowels, and aspirate.		ا	ا	ا	ا	الف	alif	a
		٨	٨	٢	ه	ها	ha	h
		ي	ي	ﻴ	ﻳ	ﻴﺎ	ya	y, i, e
		و	و	و	و	واو	waw	w, u, o
Gutturals	hard	ﻚ*	ﻚ	ﻜ	ﻛ	ﻛﺎف	kap	k
	soft	ﻚﺂ	ﻚﺂ	ﻜﺂ	ﻛﺂ	ﮔﺎ	ga	g
	nasal	ﻎ	ﻎ	ﻜ	ﻛ	ﻍ	nga	ng
Palatals	hard	ﺢ	ﺤ	ﻜ	ﺠ	ﺠﺎ	cha	ćh
	soft	ﺢ	ﺢ	ﺤ	ﺠ	ﺠﻴﻢ	jim	j
	nasal	ﺚ	ﺚ	ﻴ	ﻳ	ﻴﺎ	ña	ñ
Dentals	hard	ﺖ	ﺖ	ﻴ	ﻳ	ﺘﺎ	ta	t
	soft	ﺪ	ﺪ	ﺪ	ﺪ	ﺪﺍل	dal	d
	nasal	ﻦ	ﻦ	ﻴ	ﺟ	ﻧﻮﻥ	nun	n
Labials	hard	ﻒ	ﻒ	ﻴ	ﻳ	ﻓﺎ	pa	p
	soft	ﺐ	ﺐ	ﻴ	ﻳ	ﺑﺎ	ba	b
	nasal	ﻢ	ﻢ	ﻴ	ﻣ	ﻣﺎ	ma	m
Liquids		ﺭ	ﺭ	ﺭ	ﺭ	ﺭﺍ	ra	r
		ﻝ	ﻝ	ﻝ	ﻝ	ﻟﻢ	lam	l
Sibilant		ﺱ	ﺱ	ﺴ	ﺳ	ﺳﻴﻢ	sim	s

* Including ق when used as a substitute for this letter.

21. The Arabs divide the letters of their Alphabet into two classes—solar and lunar.

The solar letters are :—

ت ث د ذ ر ز س ش ص ض ط ظ ل ن

The lunar letters are :—

ا ب ح ج خ ح غ ع ف ق ك م و ي ه

This classification is of little use in Malay, and is only here given for the purpose of one feature of pronunciation in Arabic phrases to be explained later (Par. 106).

22. The diacritical points are integral parts of the letters, and are as inseparable therefrom as the dot over the 'i' or the cross stroke of the 't' in the Roman letters.

23. It will be remarked that the letters are written from right to left and joined, but that the letters ا د ذ ر ز and و have this distinguishing feature, that, although all of them may be joined to the letters, other than them, preceding them in words, yet when correctly written, they cannot be join-ed to letters following them.

24. The ك when final or isolated is written without the long upper stroke, but is accompanied by a miniature of the same letter in its initial or medial form (ك), to distinguish it from ل l, but this miniature letter must not be mistaken for the mark *hamzah* (ء), which it nearly resembles, nor should it accompany the letter if the long upper stroke be used. The letter ك g having been formed by the addition of 3 dots to ك k, the miniature ك k accompanies that letter also in a similar way.

25. Besides the varieties of form and combination above exhibited, there are many others in practice, which will be easily acquired from inspection of Malay writings. Some produced by haste, others by capricious license of the pen, such as an unindented slanting stroke for the س *s*, a curved stroke or semicircle instead of two dots over or under the letter, or the slight inversion of the extremity of ل *l*, in place of the final ه *h*, which latter is likewise in several shapes made to connect, but irregularly, with د ذ ر ز and و. The same letter in headings is sometimes found in the ornamental form. The combination of ل *l* with ا *a* is also written لا ، لا or لا، forming merely the syllable *la*.

26. In reading from manuscript it is very important to mark well the diacritical points or dots, called نقطة *noktah* or تيتق *ti-tek*.

27. We have said that a certain number of the letters are unnecessary in the primitive Malay, and the sounds which these letters represent in Arabic are nearly as foreign to a native Malay, as they are to us, and a wide divergence in the pronunciation of such letters will be met with. The tables above give an approximate pronunciation, but some of the letters require a little explanation.

ث *ths* the sound given to this letter by the Arabs is something like our 'th' (as in 'kith'), but is more of a hissing. Malays commonly pronounce it *s*.

ح *h* a strong guttural aspirate proceeding direct from the lungs. Malays do not usually aspirate it so strongly.

خ *kh* a strong guttural; usually modified by the Malays.

ص *s* is by the Arabs strongly articulated; the Malays render it simply *s*.

ض *dl* the strong emphatic *d* of the Arabs; by the Malays sounded *l* or *dl*.

ط *t* is in the mouth of an Arab strong and emphatic, but with the Malays only an ordinary *t*, they generally employ it to render 't' in a European word, particularly in proper names.

ظ *tl* has a peculiar sound with the Arabs, but Malays give it the value of *tl* or *l*.

ع *ain* indicates a guttural sound which is not imitated by the Malays, with whom this is a vague sign, or mere fulcrum to carry a vowel, as in عرب *àrab* 'Arab' عادة *àdat* 'custom' علمو *èlmu* 'knowledge' عيسي *ì-sa* Jesus عمر *ùmur* 'life'.

غ *gh* or *ghr* with the Arabs a strong guttural, but by the Malays usually pronounced *g* or *r*.

ف *f*. The sound of *p* being foreign to the Arabs, as *f* is to the Malays, there is often a confusion between the two, the Malays giving it either sound, in fact ف *p* is with them much more frequently written with one *noktah* than with three, and the great tendency is to give it always the sound of *p*. In the same way ك *k* is sometimes confounded with گ *g*, and also, though more rarely, ج *j* with چ *ch*, and ن *n* with ڠ *ng*.

ق *k* with the Arabs is a guttural, stronger than ك *k*, but less strong than خ *kh*. The Malays usually pronounce it

ك *k* and, when final in a word, commonly substitute it for that letter.

28. The final *k* in Malay words varies considerably in different parts in the value assigned to it. In the Straits Settlements it is nearly silent, or only serves to cut short the vowel sound which precedes it. In Sumatra and Java generally it is distinctly sounded, whilst in Borneo the sound is very hard and بَيْق *bayk* is pronounced as broadly as ' pike, spike, like '.

29. In words derived from the Arabic the final ة *h* is often found surmounted by two *noktah* (ة) , and the Malays then usually give it the value of *t*, notwithstanding that the Arabs only so pronounce it when it is followed by a word which forms a complement to the word in which it occurs. The Malays call it تا قنجيع *ta panjang* or ' long *t* ', and often use it incorrectly in place of the ordinary ت *t*. When followed by a suffixed particle. it being no longer final, becomes an ordinary ت *t*.

———

SECTION VIII.

DIVISION AND USE OF THE LETTERS.

30. The Malays like the Arabs call the letters of the Alphabet حرف *huruf* * (Ar. sing. حَرْف *har'f* pl. حروف *huráf*), and consider them all consonants,† and only moveable, or susceptible of sound, by means of vowels, which, as we shall proceed to explain, are supplemental to the letters, and are represented by certain signs placed above or below them, to indicate the vocal sound with which they should be articulated. It is as if one wrote in English M̊ N̈ M N T̂ L for ' monumental '. It is very important to bear this in mind.

Corollary : To represent an articulated isolated sound both a letter and a vowel sign ought to be used.

31. The letters are divided into حرف كرس *huruf k'ras* or ' strong letters,' and حرف لمه *huruf l'mah* or ' weak letters'. The first class comprises all the letters, except ا *alif*, و *waw*, and ي *ya*, which three form the second class.

32. The weak letters are employed in two distinct capacities. Firstly, they may be employed as simple consonants, like the strong letters, and in this state, they can only receive movement, by the application of the vowel signs, any of which may be borne upon them. They are then termed like the remainder of the letters moveable, or by the Malays حرف برباريس *huruf b'r-ba-ris* meaning ' letters carrying a

---

* The Malays do not indicate the plural or singular by declension, and a large proportion of the Arabic words adopted into Malay have been taken in the plural form, in accordance with the general tendency in the language, to treat the substantives as primarily rather general, or plural, in their signification, than singular, unless defined in the latter number by a numeral or the context.

† This term though not quite accurate is used for want of a better.

vowel sign.'* In this state ا *alif* has of itself no sound,
but serves as a mere fulcrum to carry a vowel, as if one wrote
A M P̈ D N T for 'impudent,' or Ä N F̊ S T N for 'un-
fasten', and hence by the application of the different vowels,
ا may in turn represent, either of the sounds *a*, ', *i*, *e*, *u*, or *o*,
and ي *ya* and و *waw* correspond to our letters ' y ' and
' w', when not employed as vowels, and may, by the application of different vowels, in turn represent respective-
ly, *ya*, *y'*, *yi*, *ye*, *yu*, or *yo*, and *wa*, *w'*, *wi*, *we*, *wu*, or *wo*.

33. Secondly, these three letters may be quiescent or in a
state of repose, and then they cannot receive the vowel signs,
but may be treated themselves as mere vowels. In this state
they cannot be initial, either in a word, or syllable, but
must follow a حرف بربارس *huruf b'r-ba-ris* or moveable letter,
and if the vowel borne upon such letter has a sound corresponding to that of the quiescent weak letter, such two
sounds coalesce, and form a long vowel. In this state the
quiescent weak letter is called by the Malays حرف مد *huruf*
madd meaning ' extension letter.' چنج حرف ارتين مد حرف برنام
b'r-na-ma huruf madd arti-ña huruf panjang ' named *huruf*
madd meaning long letters'. But the quiescent weak letter
may follow a letter, bearing a vowel of a different nature to
the weak letter, in which case they cannot coalesce, but
have an effect which may be described as, either, the formation of a heterogeneous vowel or diphthong, or, the causing of
the weak letter to revert to its character of consonant, and

* This term does not include the orthograpical mark *jazm*, which is the
negation of the vowel.

close the syllable. In this state the weak letter is called
حرف برجزم *ḥuruf b'r-jazm*, meaning 'letter carrying the
orthographical mark جزم *jazm* (͟),' which, as we shall see
is the negation of the vowel. Ex., ب *b* carrying the vowel *a*
and forming the syllable بَ *ba* or $\overset{a}{B}$ is followed by ا *alif*, here,
the vowel and the ا being of the same nature, their sounds
coalesce, and form a long vowel بَا *ba* or $\overset{a}{B}A$, and the ا is
حرف مد *ḥuruf madd*. But if the syllable بَ *ba* is followed by
و as in بَو *baw* or $\overset{a}{B}W$, then the vowel and the و being of different natures cannot coalesce, but form a diphthong *baw*, and
the و is then حرف برجزم *ḥuruf b'r-jazm*. These matters will
however be more readily understood, when the use of the
vowels has been explained (*see* Par. 35).

34. The vowels may be described as the life of the consonants, for, without a vowel, the consonant cannot exist as a
sound. If the reader will attempt to articulate *b* without
a vowel, he will find that the nearest approach he can make
to it is '*b* or *b*' (compare Par. 49 as to the inherent vowel),
(sibilant letters appear to be exceptions, but will be found
to be in the same category, if the sound be analyzed). It
will be observed that a consonant can be articulated, in
cutting short a preceding vowel, as in *ab*, or, in opening a
vowel following it, as in *ba*, and this is the distinction between حرف برجزم *ḥuruf b'r-jazm* and حرف برارس *ḥuruf b'r-
ba-ris*, for both must be considered consonants, and the description of 'moveable by the application of vowels' is hardly
sufficiently comprehensive, but would be more accurately rendered 'susceptible of articulated sound by the application to
them of, or of them to, vowels.'

SECTION IX.

VOWELS.

35. We have already remarked that by vowels both Malays and Arabs understand certain supplementary signs, placed above or below the letters, and indicating the vocal sound with which they should be pronounced, or by which the letters are rendered moveable. They are called by the Arabs حركات *harakāt* (plural of حركة *harakat*) signifying ' movement ', and by the Malays either بارس *ba-ris* ' lines ', or سنجات *sinja-ta* · weapons ' (perhaps from a resemblance to lances in rest).*

36. These signs are three in number :—

فتحة *fat-ḥah* or بارس دانس *ba-ris di-a-tas* ' upper stroke '

كسرة *k'srah* or بارس دباوه *ba-ris di-ba-wah* ' lower stroke ',

ضمة *dlammah* or بارس دهداڤن *ba-ris di-hada-pan* ' front stroke '.

Each of these signs has two distinct sounds.

37. فتحة *fat-ḥah* consists of a short diagonal stroke, placed over a letter, and sloping downwards from right to left.

The first sound of فتحة *fat-ḥah* is *a*, as in ككل *kakal* ' eternal ', قَدَ *pada* ' at '.

The second sound is ' as in the first syllables of كنڤ *g'nap* ' whole ', دندم *d'ndam* ' desire.' It is this sound which the Malays usually, and it would appear more correctly, give to فتحة *fat-ḥah* open and final as in رَأَس *ra-s'* ' feel ', كَاتَ *ka-t'* ' say '. All writers on Malay agree in assigning this sound to the فتحة *fat-ḥah* and

---

* In many of the languages of the Indian Archipelago, though not in Malay, nasal sounds are also represented by adjuncts to the letters.

with reason, for when, as we shall see later, the position of the مد حرف ḥuruf madd in such words changes to the ultimate syllable of the radical the vowel reverts from the second to the first sound of فتحة fat-hah, ex. gr., مرساعي m'rasa-i 'to feel', and ڤركتاعن p'r-kata-an 'words, speech', but the sound is in itself indefinite (see Par. 49), and, but for this peculiarity in Malay, would be no more assignable to one, than to another class of vowel.

38. كسرة k'srah is a sign similar in form to the preceding, but placed under the letter.

Its first sound is *i* as in دندڠ dinding ' screen ', چنچين chinchin ' ring,' بيني bi-ni ' wife.'

The second sound is *e* as in ڤاتق pa-tek ' slave ', نينق ne-nek ' grandparent.'

Both sounds of كسرة k'srah appear in تيتق ti-tek 'drop,' ڤيله pi-leh ' choose.'

39. ضمة dlammah takes the form of a small و waw, and though supposed to be placed over, and a little in front (i. e., to the left) of the letter, it is in practice placed directly over it.

Its first sound is *u* as in أندر undur ' to recede,' تنتت tuntut ' to demand.'

The second sound is *o* as in ڤندق pondok ' hut ', كندق gondok ' goitre, wen.'

Both sounds of ضمة dlammah appear in. بوسق bu-sok ' stinking ', توتر to-tur ' talk.'

40. It will be remarked that the sounds of these three signs are homogeneous with those of the three weak letters ا, ي, and و, when quiescent, and the reader will under-

stand that, upon the principle already enunciated (Par. 33), a
مد حرف‌ *huruf madd* or 'long vowel' is formed, by the
coalition of فَنْحَة *fat-hah* with ا as in تَاڠَن *ta-ngan* 'hand';
or of كسرة *k'srah* with ي as in تِيݢ *ti-ga* 'three', ديس
de-sa 'village'; or of ضمة *dlammah* with و as in بوت *bu-ta*
'blind', نوبة *no-bat* 'drum of State.' And that, when the
vowel sign is followed by, or is placed over, a weak
letter, the sound of which is dissimilar or heterogeneous
to that of the sign, the result is a diphthong, whether
at the beginning of a syllable when the weak letter is برباريس
b'r-ba-ris, as in يڠ *yang* 'which', يوت *yu-ta* 'a million',
ورت *w'rta* 'news', and وِرڠ *wi-rang* 'sombre', or at the end
of it when it is برحزم *b'r-jazm*, in which case we should
prefer to describe it as making the weak letter revert
to its character of consonant, as in ذاكي *pa-kay* 'to use',
دامي *da-may* 'peace', اغكو *ang-kaw* 'you', كيلو *ki-law*
'shining'. From this the reader will understand why
the letters 'ay' and 'aw' have been selected to represent
the diphthongal sounds nearly similar to those in 'buy'
and 'cow', even at the risk of their being mistaken for
the sounds represented by those letters in the words 'pay',
and 'flaw', instead of 'ai' and 'au', which would perhaps
better convey the sounds to an English reader, and the advantage of the selection will be further seen, when the changes in
the orthography of a radical word, caused by the suffixed particles ءي *i* and ءن *an*, are commented on (Par. 117).

41. Custom has justified the insertion in certain cases of

both the weak letters quiescent, as in جاوه *jawh* 'far', باﯦق *bayk* 'good.' FAVRE treats these words as bi-syllabic and renders them *jawuh* and *bayik* (though he gives the alteratives *jāuh* and *baik*), but this is misleading as to the pronunciation. Another analysis of these words is to consider the *alif* as برﯥارس *b'r-ba-ris,* and the words written thus جاوه and باﯦق and consisting of the syllables جَ *ja,* and أُوه *uh,* and ﯥ *ba* and إﯦق *ik,* respectively, but this is not only without authority in Malay, but involves the breach of more than one rule, and would have the effect of removing the accent from the *ā.* One educated Malay, whom the writer consulted, considered that the *alif* should be followed by ء (همزة *hamzah*), at least in the derivative forms of these words, the ء representing a deleted ا *alif* برﯥارس *b'r-ba-ris,* and this would seem to be the correct solution of the difficulty, and to be the practice of the Arabs to represent similar sounds, and to be recognized by the Malays in writing certain Arabic words, as عجائيب *àja-ib* 'wonders, marvels', and فائيده *fa-i-dah* ' benefit, advantage', بهوا سسغگهن عجائيب حكايت ايت *bahwa s'sung-guh-ña àja-ib hika-yat i-tu* ' though verily marvellous be that story ', اد سوات فائيده يغبسر *ada s'wa-tu fa-i-dah yang b'sar* 'there is one great advantage.' It is not difficult to find instances of Malay words so written, and in the same book, and on the same page, as the latter of the two examples given is found, تغگل دالم ﯥرماﯦنن يغ سﯦا ٢ *tinggal da-lam p'r-ma-i-nan yang sia-sia* ' remain (occupied) in profitless amusements', and later ادڤون طبعتمو ايت برلاﯦنن سكالي *ada-pun tabiàt-mu i-tu b'r-la-i-nan s'ka-li* ' now your nature is entirely different' (طبيعة *tabi-ảh* Ar.). And so also كاويل *kayl* 'a fishing line,' is often written with ء, as also its derivatives مغاويل *m'ng-ayl* 'to fish' and ثغاويل *p'ng-ayl* 'a fisherman', سورغ‌ر ثغاويل *s'o-rang-o-rang p'ng-ayl* 'a single fisher', ثكرجاءنئ ايت دءن مغاويل دان منجلا *p'k'rja-an-ña i-tu d'ngan m'ng-ayl dan m'n-ja-la* (منجال) 'his occupation was fishing with line and fishing with net' (*see* also Par. 91 below), and the employment of ء before the particle وي (end of Par. 115 below) appears to proceed upon a similar principle though the separate vowels are more distinctly articulated in this case.

42. In certain instances the vowels of the diphthong are found divided by the letter ه *h*, as in تاهو *ta-hu* 'know', ماهو *ma-hu* 'want', but the pronunciation hardly justifies this, and the more modern practice (which it is submitted is still less correct) is to write تاو and ماو. The separation is retained in ڤراهو *pra-hu* 'a vessel', but without much reason, and in باهو *ba-hu* 'shoulder', probably to distinguish it from باو *baw* 'odour'. In the derivative forms of تاو and ماو the ه is nearly always found, as in ثغتهوءن *p'ng-tahu-an* 'knowledge', كمهوءن *ka-mahu-an* 'will'.

43. In a few instances the vowel signs are found doubled, but only in words of Arabic origin, the effect upon the pronunciation is that the vowel is closed by a sound of *n*; for instance محمد *muhammad* becomes محمد *muhammadan*, محمد *muhammadin*, and محمد *muhammadun*. This form is called تنوين *tanwin* or بارس دو *ba-ris du-wa* and in English 'nunnation'.

44. The reader will now begin to understand why it is difficult, without a fairly extensive knowledge of the language, to read from Malay as it is usually written, viz., omitting the whole of these signs. As an illustration, a some- what exaggerated instance is subjoined, in the shape of a puzzle or catch, which even a Malay would require some thought to decipher :—

وقت تمبق تەمق دنەمق اورغ برتمبق دان برتمبق

But if the vowel signs be employed, the difficulty would dis- appear—

وَقْتُ تَمْبق تَمْبق دنَمبق اُورَغ برتَمبق دَان برتَمبق

waktu tumbuk tembok di tumbuk o-rang b'r-tombak dan b'r-tim- bak ' at the time of pounding the walls men fought, stabbing and shooting.'

45. These remarks will also explain how the practice has arisen of employing the weak letters, in the place of the omitted vowel signs, and they are so employed, at the pre- sent day, to a very large extent, and the more ignorant the writer, the more frequent is their recurrence, and in positions in which the pronunciation will not admit of the employment of a long vowel. The spelling of Malay is, at the present day, most arbitrary in this respect (*see* Pars. 138 *et seq.*).

46. There appears to be one position, in which, upon the principle *communis error facit jus*, their employment must be considered compulsory, and this is in words terminating with an open syllable, having the vowel sound of كَسْرَة *k'srah*, or ضَمَّة *dlammah*, and so مَاتِي *ma-ti* ' dead ' is written for مَات , بَاتُو , دَنْت *ba-tu* 'stone ' for بَات , نَنتي *nanti* ' wait' for

تلقّو *t'ntu* 'certain' for نَمَت, but in these cases the ي or و must not be considered as حرف مد *ḥuruf madd* or 'long vowel,' but as a mere substitute for the vowel sign. This convention does not extend to the employment of ا for فتحة *fat-ḥah* and such words as مات *ma-ta* 'the eye', كات *ka-ta* 'to say', منت *minta* 'to ask', should not be written with a final ا.

47. But if the penultimate syllable be open and short, the weak letter should be written, and considered حرف مد *ḥuruf madd* or 'long vowel', as in كنا *k'na* 'to touch', اندرا *ind'ra* (name), ترا *t'ra* 'printed, marked,' بري *b'ri* 'give', سري *s'ri* 'glory', سرو *s'ru* 'call, cry out', تبو *t'bu* 'sugar cane' (compare Pars. 55 and 93).

48. The comments upon the vowel signs would be incomplete without noticing an adjunct to the signs كسرة *k'srah* and ضمّة *dlammah*, called ميم عمال *mīm-ima-la* found in some old editions of the *Korān*, and described by ROBINSON. It has been shown that each of these signs has two sounds, and to distinguish which of these sounds the sign represents, the ميم عمال *mīm-ima-la* was invented; its form is that of a small م, and placed over the letter and its vowel mark, it signifies that the vowel sign has in such case its second sound, as in فندق *pondok* 'hut or shed', بنتڠ *benteng* 'battery'. Though so rare as to be almost unknown, the great utility of the mark seems to plead strongly for its recognition, for, without it, or something in its place, written Malay can never adequately convey the pronunciation of the

words, nor will it be possible to preserve any correct native record of the language, thus دندڠ *dinding* 'a screen' cannot be distinguished from دندڠ *dendeng* 'dried meat', nor بورڠ *bu-rong* 'a bird' from بورڠ *bo-rong* 'wholesale', etc.

49. To render Malay orthography complete, however, it would be also necessary to distinguish between the two sounds of فتحة *fat-ḥah*, and subjoined is ROBINSON'S note upon the subject :—" Were it allowable for a foreigner "to suggest an improvement, it would not be difficult to re- " move the inconvenience, which is felt in consequence of " there being no orthographical character by which one " sound of *fat-ḥah*, may be distinguished from the other. The " *fat-ḥah* or *baris di-a-tas* might be employed exclusively to " express the second (first *) sound of that vowel, as it is " heard in فنتس *pantas*, while its first (second *) sound " might be indicated by the total absence of a vowel, as " in the two following words بسر *basar* (*b'sar*) بنر " *banar* (*b'nar*). As the first (second *) sound of " the *fat-ḥah* is doubtless that vowel sound, which, in " many of the oriental languages, is considered as inherent " in the consonant, and therefore termed the inherent vowel, " the method here recommended is simply that which is " adopted in the Sungskrit, and its cognate languages. In " these languages no character is made use of to express the " inherent vowel, except at the commencement of a syllable,

---

* In this book.

" an exception which cannot apply to the Malay. Many
" syllables therefore consist of nothing but a simple
" consonant, but in which the inherent vowel is of course
" understood to be included * * * *. When it is consi-
" dered, too, that several languages ofthe Archipelago, to
" which the Malay bears a close affinity, have alphabets, and
" a system of orthography, formed upon the Sungskrit model,
" there seems no serious objection against making ·the
" Malay, though it has assumed a foreign dress, conform
" in this particular to the good old custom of its near rela-
" tives * * * * if the * * * * method here proposed * * * *
" were to be adopted, the Roman character might be laid
" aside * * * *, and Dr. MARSDEN might then present the
" world with another edition of his Dictionary, without the
" labour of writing every word in two different characters. "

SECTION X.

ORTHOGRAPHICAL MARKS.

50. These as here given are six in number :—

جزم *jazm*, مدة *maddah*, تشديد *t'shdīd*, وصلة *waslah*,
همزة *hamzah*, and اثك *angka*.

51. جزم *jazm* signifies 'cutting', and is called by
the Malays تند ماتي *tanda ma-ti*, or بارس ماتي *ba-ri
mɔ-ti*. Its form is ◦, °, or ·, and it is placed over a letter, in
the rank of the vowel signs. Its power is to indicate that th
letter, over which it is placed, has no vowel sound, of which
this mark is the negation, in other words it closes the syllable
as in تڠڬڶ *pang-gil* 'to call', لنجت *lanjut* 'to pro
long'. It can be placed over any letter (with the exceptio
perhaps of ڠ *ña*), capable of receiving a vowel sound * (se
Pars. 33 and 34 above). Malays rarely use it, notwithstanc
ing that it might be extremely useful in writing certai
words, like بوت *bu-wat* 'to do', سيڠ *si-yang* 'light
which, without the جزم *jazm*, might be taken for بوت *bu-t
'blind', and سيڠ *si-nga* 'a lion', which latter are often, i
order to distinguish them, erroneously written بوتا and سيڠا

52. مدة *maddah* or مد *madd* signifies 'prolongation
its form is ~ or ⌢ †. It is placed over a quiescent weak letter
in the rank of the vowel signs, and marks a long vowel. It i
for this purpose applied by the Malays only to ا initia
when representing the long vowel *ā* as a separate syllable

---

* It has nevertheless been contended that each *huruf madd* should bear this mark
† The Malays suppose that this is a perverted form of the Arabic numeral
(2), but it is more probably the Greek circumflex (ROBINSON).

It may be considered that, the pronunciation of the syllable requiring two *alifs*, one of them بربارس *b'r-ba-ris* accom-panied by the sign فتحه *fat-ḳah*, and the other حرف مد *ḥuruf madd* to prolong the vowel sound, but the rules of ortho-graphy not admitting of such a repetition, this mark is placed over the one *alif* (آ) to denote at the same time, the elision and the extension of sound, as in اَير *a-y'r* 'water'. In Malay words however the long *ā* initial, and forming a sepa-rate syllable, is much more commonly expressed by ه with the soft, or almost imperceptible, aspirate, to support the supplementary vowel, as in هاري *ha-ri* or *ā-ri* 'day ',* هايم *ha-yam* or اَيم *a-yam* 'fowl'.

53. Another form of this mark, called مدالف *maddalif,* is a small ١ *alif* placed over a letter, and indicating that such letter is followed by the long *a*, as in رحمٰن *raḥmān* 'merci-ful', which may be equally correctly written رحمان When over ى final in Arabic words, it is called مد اصل *madd-asʹl,* and implies that this letter has the sound *a*, as in تعالى *taàla* ' Most High', but the Malays, on the contrary, some-times introduce it instead of applying فتحه *fat-ḳah* to the preceding consonant, to produce the diphthong ' *ay* ', as in فاكى instead of فاكي *pa-kay* ' to use'.

54. It has been already observed (Par. 33), that a quies-cent weak letter, representing a prolongation of sound, is called حرف مد *ḥuruf madd,* and when found in the middle of a syllable (as it often is in Arabic), as the ١ in لام *lām* the

---

* The idea conveyed by this word is a period of 24 hours, from sunset to sunset.

in نُون *nūn*, and the ي in مِيم *mīm*, it is called مَدّ ضَرُورِي *madd-dlaru-ri*, or مَدّ لَازِم *madd'la-zim*. A مَدّة *maddah* might be applied to each حَرْف مَدّ *huruf madd*, but, as we have observed, the Malays rarely use it except over *alif* initial in certain words. The Arabs so employ it as in خَالِق *kha-likun* 'Creator,' مُومِنُون *mu-minu-na* 'the faithful', and خَالِيفَة *khāli-fah* 'a Caliph, or lieutenant'. They also employ it medial in a word but initial in a syllable, as in قُرَان *kur-ān* 'the Korān'. Finally مَدّة *maddah* is used over abbreviations, as مّ for عَلَيْه السَّلَام *ālayi-hi'ss'lām* 'peace be upon him', and سّ for سَسُنّگُهُن *s'sungguh-ña* 'verily'.

55. تَشْدِيد *t'shdīd* (named also شَدّ *shaddu*) signifies 're-inforcement'. Its form is ّ, and placed over a letter doubles it. It can be applied to all strong letters except غ *nga*, چ *cha*, and ث *ña*. When a strong letter is so doubled, the first joins the preceding consonant, and forms with it a closed syllable, and the second takes the vowel properly belonging to the letter, and accompanying the mark, as in تَمّة *t'mmat* 'finis', جَنّة *j'nnat* ' paradise '. The تَشْدِيد *t'shdīd* is never applied to ١, but when placed over و or ي doubles the letter so marked, the first becoming حَرْف مَدّ *huruf madd* of the preceding consonant, and forming the long vowel,*

---

* This rule admits of exceptions in Arabic words, but not, so far as we have been able to ascertain, in any native word. The exceptions in Arabic occur where the weak letter marked with *t'shdid* is preceded by a letter having a vowel heterogenous to the weak letter. In this case, as we have seen, the weak letter may be treated as a simple consonant, ex., سَيِّد *say-yid* 'Lord, master, the title assumed by certain Arabs who claim to be of the race of Muhammad. From the Malays writing مَيّة for the word pronounced *may-yat* 'a corpse,' it would appear that this peculiarity is known to them, but ' corpse ' is more correctly rendered مَيْتَة *maytah*, and Malays probably misuse the word مَيْت *may't* 'death'.

and the second becoming حرف برپارس ḥuruf b'r-ba-ris of the
next syllable, and taking the vowel sound, the sign of which
should accompany the تشديد t'shdīd, as in بوّت bu-wat
'to do', سيّغ si-yang 'light'. Were these words written
without the تشديد t'shdīd, or if its presence were not
supposed (Malays usually omitting it), they would stand
thus بووت and سييغ , here it is clear that the first
و or ي is حرف مد ḥuruf madd of the first syllable بو bu or
سي si, and the second حرف برپارس ḥuruf b'r-ba-ris beginning
the syllables وت wat and يغ yang respectively.

N. B.—It must be admitted, however, that there is a very
common practice of inserting an ا as compensation for the
omitted تشديد t'shdīd over the letter و , if فتحه fat-ḥah
should accompany that mark, and it amounts almost to an
accepted convention to write توان for توّن tu-wan 'Mr.',
لوار for لوّر lu-war 'out', توا for بوّه bu-wah 'fruit,'
for تو or توّ tu-wa ' old ', دوا for دوّ du-wa 'two,'
بواغ for بوّغ bu-wang 'cast away', جوال for جوّل ju-wal ' to
sell', and many others in a similar manner, but the practice
is not so common in the case of the other weak letter, and
بير bi-yar ' allow ' is never written بيار , nor ديم di-yam
' dwell, remain, be still ' ديام , nor لير li-yar ' wild ' ليار,
but نيّر ñi-yor ' cocopalm '' is usually written نيور , and چيّم
chi-yum 'to kiss' چيوم . The تشديد t'shdīd is not always audible
in pronunciation, and especially where it would produce any
harshness, and, but for the fact that this use of the Roman

letters might mislead as to the proper Arabic letters to be used, it would be better to write *bwat* or *buat* than *bu-wat* for بوت (*see* Appendix B).

56. In the formation of derivatives, as will be hereafter explained, the حرف مد *ḥuruf madd* is often found in a different position to that in which it was in the radical word, but if such letter should, in the radical, have borne the mark تشديد *t'shdīd*, that mark is, in such case, lost in the derivative, but the loss is equivalent to the deletion of so much only of the duplication, as consists of حرف مد *ḥuruf madd*. Thus from بوت *bu-wat* ' to do ' = بووت is formed قروبواتن *p'r-buwa-tan* 'the thing done'; here the و as the first part of the duplication, and حرف مد *ḥuruf madd* of the radical, is omitted in the derivative, and there remains only و *wa* بربارس *b'r-ba-ris*, following بِ *bu*, and ا as حرف مد *ḥuruf madd* appears in the penultimate of the derivative word.

57. It must be noted that a حرف مد *ḥuruf madd* formed by the application of تشديد *t'shdīd* to و, invariably gives it the first sound of ضمة *dlammah*, that is *u* (not *o*), and by its application to ي the first sound of كسرة *k'srah*, that is *i* (not *e*). As some difficulty may occur as to when تشديد *t'shdīd* may be applied to و and ي the following rule has been formulated :—" When they in a radical are followed by a حرف مد *ḥuruf madd* they cannot take this mark ", ex. بياس *biya-sa* 'accustomed', بواي *buwa-ya* 'crocodile'. No further comment on this mark is necessary, for the Malays

rarely use it, except over the word الله *allah* 'God', and it is a refinement introduced from a language, with which the Malay has little in common; but its presence must be supposed to account for the traditional spelling of certain words, such as اي *i-ya* or دي *di-ya* 'he, she, they', سدي *s'di-ya* 'ready', ملي *muli-ya* 'worthy', and a number of others in addition to those already given (Par. 55).

58. وصله *waslah* or وصل *was'l* signifies 'union'. Its form is ‏ ‎and placed over ا renders it mute, allowing a junction between the preceding, and succeeding letters. It is only used in Arabic phrases, and mainly in the definitive particle ال *al*, as in كتاب النبي *kita-bunnabi* 'book of the Prophet' روح القدس *ro-ḥul-kudus* 'Holy Ghost', رسول الله *rasu-lullah* 'apostle of God', رسول الله *rasu-lillah* ' of the apostle of God '.

59. The first syllable of the word الله *allah*, which is an abbreviation, is the article ال *al*, and the second part إله *illah* 'God' thus signifying 'The God', 'The One God'. It is for this reason that, when a possessive noun or pronoun follows it, the article is omitted, as in اله ابراهيم *illah ibra-hīm* 'God of Abraham', الهك *illah-ku* 'My God', اله كامي *illah ka-mi* 'Our God'. We must however caution the reader, that the genitive in Malay being formed by position, and not by declension, these forms though correct in Malay would not be good Arabic, and in the first instance quoted, a كسرة *k'srah* would be placed

under the final ي , to denote the genitive case كَتَبُ النَّبِيِّ

, *kita-bunnabi-yi* (*see* Par. 106 below). Nor must the reader in any case assume that the Arabic words occurring from time to time are grammatically correct Arabic.

60. همزة *hamzah* is the most used by the Malays of all the orthographical marks ; its form is ء being merely the letter ع *ain* reduced in size. It is either an appendage to ا *alif* برباس *b'r-ba-ris*, properly accompanying its vowel sign, and placed between the letter (if initial) and the sign, and therefore either above or below it, or it is the representative or substitute for the letter. So close is the connection between them, that the Malays say in speaking of the *alif*, اقبيل برڤارس همزه نمان جكلو تياد برڤارس الف نمان *apabi-la b'r-ba-ris hamzah nama-ña jikalaw tiya-da b'r-ba-ris alif nama-ña* 'when it (*alif*) bears a vowel sign its name is *hamzah* when it has no vowel sign its name is *alif*'. As an appendage to *alif* it reduces the latter to a sort of imperceptible aspirate, the only power of which is to give movement to the. vowel sound accompanying it, thus أَبْ *ab* إِبْ *ib* أُبْ *ub.*

61. In Malay, however, where the weak, or vowel letters, are sparingly employed, the chief use of ء is to express the elision of *alif* برڤارس *b'r-ba-ris*, medial in a word, but at the commencement of a syllable, whether following one of the three weak letters ا و or ي quiescent, or a consonant rendered mute by جزم *jazm*, or a prefixed particle consisting of an open syllable. These instances mostly occur in derivatives formed by annexing particles as will be hereafter explained, ex. gr.,

فكرجاءن *p'k'rja-an* 'performance', كَنتَنُوْن *ka-t'ntu-an* ' certainty ', كَننتِيْن *ka-nanti-an* ' expectation ', كَنمڤت *ka-ampat* ' the fourth '. Universal custom at the present day however retains the *alif*, when following either of the particles د *di*, بر *b'r*, بل *b'l*, تر *t'r*, ڤر *p'r*, or قل *p'l*, as in داڠكت *di-angkat* 'lifted', داأمبق *di-ombak* ' on the waves', برأوله *b'r-o-leh* ' to possess', ترأتام *t'r-ata-ma* 'most excellent', ڤرأراكن *p'r-ara-kan* ' procession', ڤلأجارن *p'l-aja-ran* ' lesson, instruction ' (see Pars. 84, 104 and 105).

62. ء supplies the elision of أ before و or ي at the beginning of a word when س *sa* or *s'* (a contraction of اس *asa* 'unity, oneness, one, a, an ') is prefixed, as سؤرڠ *s'o-rang* ' a man ', سئيكور *s'-e-kor* ' a tail ', as well as by custom in certain instances, as مغكؤجر *mak'u-j'r* for ملك اوجر *maka u-j'r* 'and he said', مريكئيت *marik-i-tu* for مريك ايت *mari-ka i-tu* ' they, those people '. It also sometimes marks the elision of ه *h* initial, when the particles مغ *m'ng* and ڤغ *p'ng* are prefixed, as in مغأمبر *m'ng-ambur* ' to sow, scatter ', but the retention of the ه seems preferable, as مغهمبر *m'ng-ham-bur* even though no trace of the aspirate remains in the pronunciation of the derivative word. It is used generally whenever such elisions occur.

63. Its use is advocated to mark the elision ك *k* initial, when that letter is dropped for euphony on the application of the particles مغ *m'ng* and ڤغ *p'ng*, as in مغؤرجا *m'ng-'rja* 'to work ' a derivative formed from كرج *k'rja* ' work '. It is sometimes so used by the Malays, but not generally, though

there are strong reasons for its employment.* The particles
م٘ڠ *m'ng* and ڤ٘ڠ *p'ng* appear to be closed syllables, and if
ء be not employed in the instance given, it becomes necessary to divide the م٘ڠ *m'ng*, and consider the word as مڠرج
m'-ng'r-ja, this is inconsistent with the pronunciation, which
is *m'ng-'r-ja* the first and second bèing closed syllables, and
this being so, the opening vowel of the second must, as we
shall hereafter see, be borne on a letter or its substitute, and
the proper mark is evidently ء . To write the syllable alone
it must appear either أر or ءر   and we shall see that ا is in-
admissible. This will be still more apparent from another
instance, from كنل *k'nal* 'to know', is formed مڠنل *m'ng-'-nal*
here without ء   the word would probably be pronounced
m'ng-nal, which results in the omission of an entire syllable.
This reasoning is controverted by FAVRE, and he has the
support of the more general practice of Malay writers.†

64. Sometimes, placed after a weak letter terminating a
word, it indicates that such letter takes the place of the
nearly silent ق or ك, as in ادي *a-de* for ادق *a-dek* 'younger
sister, or brother ', ماماء *ma-ma* for مامق *ma-mak* ' uncle,
aunt' انچيء *inche* for انچق *inchek* 'Mr.', and sometimes, placed
over a weak letter terminating a word, it indicates that such
letter is a substitute only for the vowel sign, as in كاكي *ka-ki*
'foot' for كاك , in which cases it is called همزه ماتي *hamzah
ma-ti*, but these uses of it are rare.

---

65. Further ء marks abbreviations, as in ڏاء *ta* for تِيٳد *tiya-da* or تيدق *ti-dak* ' not ', and ڏه *na* for هندق *handak* ' wish, intend'. تاواكن قيسغ برٻوه دوا كالي *ta akan pi-sang br-bu-wah da-wa ka-li* 'The banana does not bear fruit twice' (Prov.).

66. Lastly ء as a substitute should be written slightly above the line of the letters, but otherwise as near as circumstances will permit to the place of the letter, the elision of which it marks, and not in the rank of vowel signs and orthographical marks, ex., كندٳءن *ka-ada-an* ' existence '.

67. اڠك *angka* the Arabic numeral ٢ (2). Used as an orthographical mark, and placed after a word, and in line with the letters, it signifies that the word to which it is applied is repeated, as بايق٢ *bayk-bayk* 'very good, very well'. The repetition of words is very frequent in Malay, and is usually indicated by this mark, but its use will be better understood, from the notes on duplicated words below (Pars. 127 *et seq.*). It is sometimes met with as the Arabic numeral ٣ (3), signifying that the word is repeated three times مك سڬل خلايق ايتڤون مڠڠكتكن تاڠن۳ سراي مڠٳتكن امين۳ *maka s'gala khala-ik i-tupun m'ng-angkat-kan ta-ngan-ña s'ra-ya m'ng-ata-kan amin amin amin* 'and all the congregation (creatures) thereupon lifted up their hands whilst exclaiming Amen! Amen! Amen! '.

68. The vowel signs and orthographical marks have been treated at considerable length, but from the prominence given to them, it must not be taken, that the writing of every word,

with all its vowels, and appropriate marks, is for a moment recommended, but written Malay will never be free from ambiguity, so long as they are totally omitted. Some words are easily recognizable in this state, but many must be deciphered by the context. Some words might be distinguished as ﺗﻮﻦ *tu-wan* 'master' from ﺗﻮﻦ *tu-nu* 'burn', ﺑﻮﺕ *bu-wat* 'to do' from ﺑﻮﺕ *bu-ta* 'blind'. Proper names particularly, if unusual, ought to be written with all their vowels and orthographical marks, as also unfamiliar or foreign words.

SECTION XI.

NUMERALS.

69. THE practice of writing from right to left does not extend to the numerals, which are grouped as with us. The European numerals are very generally known, and frequently used by the Malays at the present day, but the greater proportion employ the Arabic, which are as follows :—

١	٢	٣	٤ or ٤	٥	٦
1	2	3	4	5	6
سانو	دوا	تيݢ	امڤت	ليم	انم
sa-tu	du-wa	ti-ga	ampat	li-ma	anam or 'nam

٧	٨	٩	٠	١٠
7	8	9	0	10
توجه	دلاڤن or لاڤن	سمبيلن	كوسوڠ or اڠك	سڤوله
tu-joh	dula-pan or la-pan	sambi-lan	angka or ko-sung	s'-pu-loh

١١	١٢	١٩	٢٠
11	12	19	20
سبلس	دوا بلس	سمبيلن بلس	دوا ڤوله
s'-b'las	du-wa-b'las	sambi-lan b'las	du-wa pu-loh

٢٥	25	دوا ڤوله ليم	du-wa pu-loh li-ma 'two tens, five'

١٨١	181	سراتس لاڤن ڤوله سانو	s'-ra-tus la-pan pu-loh sa-tu 'one hundred, eight tens, one'.

٤٦٧	467	امڤت راتس انم ڤوله توجه	ampat ra-tus anam pu-loh tu-joh 'four hundreds, six tens, seven'.

١٣٠٩	1309	سريبو تيݢ راتس سمبيلن	s'-ri-bu ti-ga ra-tus sambi-lan 'one thousand, three hundreds, nine'.

The name of the first numeral is a compound of اس
usa signifying ' unity, oneness, isolation', and باتو *ba-tu* or
واتو *wa-tu* 'stone', the latter word being employed merely
as a symbol of numeration ; both ساتو *sa-tu* and سوات
s'-wa-tu are in common use. Many other symbols are employed in numeration in place of باتو *ba-tu*, such as ايكر
e-kor 'tail' for animals, سدّيكر لمبو *s'-e-kor l'mbu* 'one ox', and
بوه *bu-wah* 'fruit' تيتّ بوه كفل *ti-ga bu-wah kapal* 'three
ships' توجه بواه رومه *tu-joh bu-wah ru-mah* 'seven houses'.

70. A system exists, the use of which is occasionally met
with among the Malays, and which is known to them through
the Arabic scholars, termed ابجد *abj'd*. In this the num-
bers are represented by the letters of the Arabic Alphabet in
its ancient order, as follows :—

ا	ب	ج	د	ه	و	ز	ح	ط	ي	ك	ل	م	ن
1	2	3	4	5	6	7	8	9	10	20	30	40	50

س	ع	ف	ص	ق	ر	ش	ت	ث	خ	ذ	ض	ظ	غ
60	70	80	90	100	200	300	400	500	600	700	800	900	1000

In this system the grouping is reversed ; ex. gr :—

يا	كج	قيه	شكه	غفصا
11	23	115	325	1891

but if the order be reversed, or mixed, the total remains
unchanged.

SECTION XII.

PUNCTUATION.

71. No system of punctuation, corresponding to our stops, is known in Malay. The subdivision of sentences depends almost entirely, as in our legal documents, upon the grammatical construction. This, with the fact that there is little or no declension, leads to a considerable amount of tautology. The beginnings of sentences or new subjects are, however, marked by certain conventional words mainly drawn from Arabic sources. These words are usually written in larger characters than the rest, and are employed without much regard to their actual meaning. They are called سمڤولن simpu-lan 'knottings' or ايبو ڤركتاٴن i-bu p'r-kata-an 'mothers of the discourse'.

72. The word in most common use for this purpose is the native (?) word مك maka,* which answers the purpose of, and is used with about the same frequency as, the full stop with us, though it marks the beginning, and not the end, of a sentence. It may be roughly translated 'and' or 'now', but is mostly without meaning, مك كات اورڠ maka ka-ta o-rang 'now people say' مك هاريڤون مالملم مك راج براڠكت كمالݝ maka ha-ri-pun ma-lam-lah maka ra-ja b'r-angkat ka-ma-ligay. 'The night came on. The King repaired to the palace.'

73. Beyond the mere conventional use of this word, how-

---

*The origin of this word is in doubt, CRAWFURD connects it with the Javanese *mangka*. BIKKERS gives two meanings 'now', and 'yet'. It is possible that its use is coeval with the introduction of the Arabic letters, and that it is connected with مكت *makat* 'to rest'.

ever, there are numerous instances in which a certain meaning seems attached to it بلم كرغ سواتو اعڠوتڽ ٠مك دباسهڽ لاين
b'lum kring s'wa-tu anggo-ta-ña maka di ba-sah-ña lain
' one limb is not dry before he wets another',
جكلاو توان ڤوڽ سك مك براني سهاي ماسق *jik·law tu-wan pu-ña*
suka maka b'ra-ni s'ha-ya ma-sok 'if my master wishes it, then
certainly I dare enter', اورڠ مان اين مك داڤت سمڤي كڬونڠ اين
o-rang ma-na i-ni maka da-pat sampay ka-gu-nong i-ni ' what
(manner of) man is this, that he should be able to reach this
mountain ', مك دڤراولهڽ *maka di-p'r-o-leh-ña* ' in order that
he may obtain it ' (lit. ' that it may be by him obtained ').

74. The word مك, as marking the beginning of a sentence
or paragraph, is found preceded, in an indiomatic manner, by
a number of other words and phrases, which, in their turn, may
be used without it, as سڤرمول مك *s'-b'r-mu-la maka* ' In
the first place', بهوا مك *bahwa maka* ' Whereas', حتي مك
ḥatta maka ' Thus, when that, until, in order that, according
to, therein comprised', شهدان مك *sh'hadān maka* 'Moreover,
thus it is that ', نصيحت *n'si-ḥat* ' Exhortation, a word of
advice ', كلكين *k'l'ki-yan* ' Whenever, so often as, thereupon ', اركين *arki-yan* ' Moreover, further', استميو *istime-*
wa ' Especially', ادڤون *ada-pun* ' Now ', برمول *b'r-mu-la*.
or سبرمول *s'-b'r-mu-la* ' To begin with ', بهواسڽ short for
bahwa s'sungguh-ña ' Though verily', دان *dan* ' And',
سباڬيلاڬي *s'ba-gay-lagi* ' And similarly', سباڬيڤول *s'ba-*
gay-pu-la 'And so also', سكاليڤرستوا *s'ka-li-p'r-s'tu-a* 'Former-
ly '. Besides these many other forms will be met with, ex.

القصه ملك دچرترا‌کن اورغ يغ امفون چرترا اين ملك ادا‌له *alkissat* maka di ch‘rtra-kan o-rang yang ampu-ña ch‘rt‘ra i-ni maka ada-lah. 'The narration. Now it is related by the person whose relation this is, how that there were &c.'

75. The termination of a paragraph is mostly marked by ادا‌ن *ada-ña*, and of a subject very often by تمة القصة *t‘mmat ulkissat* 'end of the story', or some high sounding Arabic phrase, such as والله اعلم بالصواب واليه المراجع والمأوب *wallahu aàlam biss‘wāb walai-hil mara-jà walma-ab.*

76. Official or formal letters mostly begin with بهو اين ورقة *bahwa i-ni warakat* 'Whereas this epistle', followed by high sounding expressions of sincerity or humility, called فُجَفُجِيٌن *puji-puji-an* or فوجي‌فوجي‌ان 'compliments', with the name, address, and titles of the person addressed, and of the sender. The opening of the subject matter of the communication is marked by such words as أمّا بعد *amma-bàdu*, or وبعدا *wabàdān*, but commonly written وبعده *wabaàdah* meaning 'after, and now, furthermore,' to which the Malays often add superfluously كمدين *k‘mdi-yan* 'after'. The date comes last, and the end of the letter is marked by such expressions as تمة الكلام *t‘mmatul-kalām* 'the end of the discourse or writing'.

———

SECTION XIII.

SYLLABLES.

77. هِجَاء *hijā* or ايج *e-ja* signifies 'letter of the Alphabet', and in Malay also 'syllable', and مغْليج *m'ng-eja* or مغْهجاء *m'ng-heja* 'to divide into its component parts, reduce to orthography, write or spell a word'.

78. Every syllable must begin with a حرف برباريس *ḥuruf b'r-ba-ris*, whether it be a strong, or a weak letter, ex., كات *ka-ta* 'to say', بسر *b'sar* 'large', أوبت *o-bat* 'medicine', يمتوان *yam-tu-wan* 'ruler', ورت *w'rta* 'news'. The only exception to this rule is when such a letter is deleted, and its place is taken by ء, همزة *hamzah*.

79. Those words, in which a long *ā* alone forms the initial syllable, as in اير *a-y'r* 'water', look at first sight like exceptions to this rule, but are not so in reality, for, as we have seen (Par. 52.), the ا should bear the mark مدة *maddah* (~) indicating that it is equal to two *alifs*, the first برباريس *b'r-ba-ris* and the second حرف مد *ḥuruf madd*, and the word being equivalent to أَيْر or هايْر.

80. The almost invariable omission by the Malays of the vowel signs, and orthographical marks, has led to the latter form being adopted for a large number of words, such as هاري *ha-ri* 'day', هالو *ha-law* 'to drive', and a very common substitution of ه *h* for ا movable, as in هيل *he-la* 'to draw', هولو *hu-lu* 'head', and many words are written indiscriminately either way, as ايم *a-yam* or هايم *ha-yam*

fowl', اولت *u-lat* or هولت *hu-lat* 'worm, maggot'
انت *unta* or هنت *hunta* 'camel'.

81. It has been stated that every Malay syllable must
begin with a حرف بربارس *huruf b'r-ba-ris*, and in those words
beginning with ا it is absolutely necessary, for the purpose of
writing derivatives correctly, to discriminate between
الف بربارس *alif b'r-ba-ris*, and الف مد *alif madd*. The
ا marked with ~ is equivalent to two *alifs*, the first
بربارس *b'r-ba-ris* or a mere fulcrum to carry the vowel
فتحة *fat-ḥah*, the sound of which is prolonged by the
second ا. Custom forbids the use of همزة *hamzah* before الف مد *alif madd* as an initial, yet such a practice
would tend to perspicuity, and obviate any difficulty as to
spelling, when a particle is prefixed; thus if instead of أجر
a-j'r 'teach', were written ءاجر, it would lead at once to
the derivative مڠاجر *m'ng-a-j'r* ' to teach ', in which the
~ is omitted. (*But see* Appendix A).

82. An *alif* initial, and not marked, nor supposed to
be marked, with ~, is بربارس *b'r-ba-ris*, and may carry
either of the vowel signs. In this case, as we have seen
(Par. 60.), Malays call it همزة *hamzah*, and it should bear
that mark, as in أرتي. *arti* 'sense, signification', أثڬن *'ngga*[n]
'to refuse', أنتڠ *untong* 'profit, gain', إنچي *incke* 'Mr.'
أنجق *unjok* 'to show, point out.' Now to follow out the
idea of replacing أ by ء, we have in the latter instance
ءنجق and this leads at once to the correct derivative

مثْلُنْجق‎ *m'ng-unjok,* and it will be observed that the ء‎
retains the vowel sign, which the آ‎ had in the radical word.

83. It will be seen, therefore, that آ‎ and ء‎ are of equal
value, but they cannot be used indiscriminately. آ‎ can in
general only be used as initial in a radical word,* and when a
particle is prefixed (other than د‎ *di,* بر‎ *b'r,* بل‎ *b'l,* تر‎ *t'r,*
ڤر‎ *p'r,* or ڤل‎ *p'l*) it disappears, and its place is taken by ء‎,
thus from أمڤت‎ *ampat* 'four' is formed كأمڤت‎ *ka-ampat*
'the fourth'; from أمڤت‎ *umpat* 'calumny' مأمڤت‎ *m'ng-*
umpat 'to calumniate'; and from انجق‎ *injak* 'trampled, trodden
down' مأنجق‎ *m'ng-injak* 'to trample down'. This explanation also accounts for the elision of آ‎ as in سؤرغ‎ *s'-o-rang* 'a
person', &c., as noticed above (Par. 62).

84. It has been before observed that custom allows the retention of آ‎ when following the particles د‎ *di,* بر‎ *b'r,* بل‎ *b'l,*
تر‎ *t'r,* ڤر‎ *p'r* and ڤل‎ *p'l,* as in براوله‎ *b'r-o-leh* 'to possess,' etc.,
but even these will be found at times in the older works
written with ء‎, as برؤله‎ and it would appear to be more
systematic so to write them.

85. From these remarks, it will be obvious that every
vowel sound must be borne upon a letter, or mark representing the elision of a letter, and there are three letters, and
one mark, which can be used for this purpose, and the sounds

---

* Compare however end of Par. 55.

of which are practically (and in the case of two of them, آ and
ء , entirely*) imperceptible. The letters are أ الف بربارس
alif b'r-ba-ris, ع *ain*, and ه *h*, and the mark is ء همزة
hamzah. Each of these may carry any of the vowel signs and
sounds, and one or other must be employed whenever it is
necessary to represent a vowel sound, not borne upon one of
the letters which has a definite and distinctive sound. It has
been already pointed out that ء is but an abbreviated ع *ain*.

86. Syllables are divided into two classes, open, and closed
syllables. It is customary to make a third class, that of mixed
syllables, but this does not appear necessary for the purposes
of this work.

87. An open, or pure, syllable is one terminating with an
open vowel sound ; of this nature are the syllables of كات
ka-ta 'to say', تيڬ *ti-ga* 'three', بڽاس *bina-sa* 'destroyed'
تيرو *ti-ru* 'copy', بواي *buwa-ya* 'crocodile'. It may be either
long, like the penultimates in these examples, or short, like
the remainder. Beyond the case of the coalescence of a vowel
sound with the weak letter quiescent, and forming حرف مد
huruf madd, there is no certain indication whether the syllable
be short, or long. An open syllable penultimate is usually
long, but from this must be excepted :—

1st.—Syllables having the vague or uncertain sound ' as

---

in كنل *k'nal* 'to recognize', بتل *b'tal* 'correct', تله *t'lah*
'past', مڠ *m'nang* 'win', لبه *l'bih* 'more', گرق *g'rak*
'move, stir', ثنت *p'nat* 'tired', سلم *s'lam* 'dive', دمم
d'mam 'fever', جرت *j'rat* 'noose', ترس *t'ras* 'through',
بكس *b'kas* 'imprint, foot-mark', ڤرت *p'rut* 'belly',
بله *b'lah* 'split', لمه *l'mah* 'weak', سكم *s'kam* 'husks,
chaff', مرق *m'rak* 'peacock', سدڠ *s'dang* 'whilst', سنڠ
s'nang 'in peace, in comfort, well off', تڤوڠ *t'pong* 'flour', and
ددق *d'dak* 'meal, the broken grain of rice'. (As noticed
above Par. 16).

2nd.—Words originally monosyllabic, but to which, in accordance with the tendency of the language, a second syllable
has been prefixed, as in أمس *'mas* from مس *mas* 'gold',
هلي *h'lay* from لي *lay* 'fold', هلڠ *h'lang* from لڠ
lang 'kite, hawk'.

3rd.—Certain foreign words, such as *ma-ligay* مالڬي
'palace', مانكم *ma-nikam* 'rubies, precious stones', كارن
ka-rana 'for, on account of'. The tendency is, however, to
assimilate such words to the Malay, and the latter is now
commonly written كران *kara-na*.

88. An open syllable ultimate is generally short, nor are
the cases, in which (as noticed above, Par. 46) modern custom
allows the use of the quiescent weak letter final, as a substitute for the vowel sign, exceptions to this rule, as in تيڤو
ti-pu 'to deceive', ڤادو *pa-du* 'solid', سرڤو *s'rbu* 'to sur-
prise', برهنتي *b'r-henti* 'to stop, be stationary', براني
b'ra-ni 'bold', بنچي *binchi* 'to hate, abhor'. But when the

penultimate has the indefinite vowel ' open, the ultimate
is generally long (*see* Par. 47).

89. A closed syllable is composed of two letters, the first
having a vowel sign, and the second rendered mute by جزم
jazm. Of this nature are both syllables of تمڤت *t'mpat*
'place', ڤڠڬل *panggil* 'to call', ڤندي *pinday* 'clever', كربو
k'rbaw 'buffalo', انتق *antok* 'drowsy', امبن *umbun* 'dew',
the first in تنتو *t'ntu* 'certain', بڠس *bangsa* 'nation,
race', the second in ايكت *i-kat* 'bind', and بوجق *bu-jok*
'flatter, soothe, persuade'.

90. No closed syllable in a native Malay word should have
a letter of prolongation of sound, or حرف مد *huruf madd.**
The breach of this rule is the most common cause of discrepancy in Malay spelling. Two words, however, are almost always written with the letter of prolongation of sound, viz., ڤون
pun 'also', and دان *dan* 'and', but even these will be found
in the older writings ڤن and دن, and more correctly, for
there is nothing in the pronunciation to justify the modern
innovation. The rule, as above stated, refers to the native
words only; in those cf foreign origin, the weak letter quiescent is often found in closed syllables, whether for the purpose
of defining the vowel sound, as in تيه *teh* (Chinese) 'tea', or
in accordance with the spelling of the language from which
such words are drawn, as in اسلم *islam* 'Islam', رسول
rasul 'apostle', امين *amin* 'Amen, so be it', and many

---

* A little careful study of the Malay pronunciation will be conclusive of the correctness of this rule when such letter is compared to the *madd la-sim* of the Arabic.

others. شهيد نم ٔن دان سورڬ اكن بالسن shahīd *(Ar.)* nama-ña dan sūrga *(Hind.)* akan ba-las-ña 'they shall be called martyr, and heaven shall be their reward'.

91. Custom allows the use of one, or even both, the weak letters in the case of certain diphthongs, and it might be considered that such words consist of two, rather than one syllable, as in the instance above given (Par. 41.) جاوه *jawh* 'far'. This appears to be the opinion of FAVRE, who writes it *jawuh* (though he adds the alternative spelling *jāuh*), and if his explanation could be accepted, it would obviate any breach of the rule as to closed syllables, and simplify the formation of derivatives. Thus by the application of the particle ءِ *i* (in accordance with the rules, which we shall proceed to deal with under the head of 'Suffixed Particles'), he would have جا *ja*, the first syllable, loose its letter of pre-longation of sound ا, and would divide the second syllable وه *wuh*, giving the و another و, as letter of prolongation of sound, and causing the ه to unite with the particle, and form with it a separate syllable هي *hi*, منجوڬوهي *m'n-jawu-hi*. This may be well as a theory, but it is not consistent with the practice of the Malays themselves, nor does the pronunciation justify the treatment of these words as dissyllables in this manner.

92. Malays appear to pronounce them as monosyllables, and generally to subject them to no change by the application of suffixed particles, except that, with the particles ن *an* and ءِ *i*, they exchange a final ق , if the word ends with

that letter, for ک , and consider the جزم *jazm* removed
from the final letter. The words of this class, at least those
which commonly receive particles, are few in number, the
chief being بايق *bayk* 'good', جاوه *jawh* 'far', لاوت *lawt*
'sea', لاين *layn* 'other', ماين *mayn* 'sport', and نايق
nayk 'to ascend', which Malays write in their derivative forms, as in ممبايكي *m'm-bay-ki* 'to repair', منجاوهي
m'n-jaw-hi 'to recede' (Fr. éloigner), لاوتن *law-tan* 'seas',
ملاينكن *m'layn-kan* 'except' (or ملينكن), برلاينن *b'r-lay-nan*
difference', قرماينن *p'r-may-nan* 'sports' (or قرميينن),
كنايكن *ka-nay-kan* 'the mounting'; and this appears to be the
orthography recognized by MARSDEN (who considered them
monosyllabic), though both ماينن , and ميينن , appear in his
Dictionary, as also ملينكن (and this is the way this word is perhaps more commonly written). These words must therefore
be treated as exceptions, and their orthography would seem
to demand that the 3rd and 4th letters in the radical should
be considered as برجزم *b'r-jazm*, as لاين لاوت جاوه بايق
ماير and نايق . The second letter would appear, by the pronunciation, to be حرف مد *huruf madd*, but to be simulta-
neously used as حرف برباريس *huruf b'r-ba-ris* to support
the second long vowel. The Malays do not appear to
have settled what sign should properly accompany this second
letter, but it is evident that, failing its being followed by ر
as mentioned above (Par. 41), something is necessary to
distinguish words of this nature from those, in which similar
letters occur, without forming a diphthong, as قوﻍ *pa-wang*

'a hunter', فِيْغ pa-yong 'an umbrella', قَايه pa-yah 'difficult', جاوا ja-wa 'Java', &c., or ساوه sawh 'anchor', from ساوه sa-wah 'paddy field'. We have seen that in some instances Malays have obviated the difficulty by making the words bisyllabic, as تاهو ta-hu 'to know', ماهو ma-hu 'to want', and instances are met with in which ع ain is used to support the second vowel مك اي ڤون ماعوله ماسوء اڬم اسلام maka i-ya pun ma-ŭ-lah ma-ro aga-ma islām 'and he was desirous of entering the religion of Islam'.

93. It was at one time considered, and enunciated as an infallible rule, that 'there is no word in the Malay language consisting only of short pure syllables', and that 'when all the syllables are open, one must contain a حرف مد huruf madd'. If this proposition be accepted as correct, and we think that theoretically it should be so, then it is necessary to account for the spelling of the words اد ada 'to be', ڤد pada 'at', مك maka 'now', اڤ apa 'what', دري d'ri 'from', اڬم agama 'religion', سڬل s'gala 'all', اتم atama 'chief, principal', سك suka 'joy', دك duka 'grief', چت chita 'sensation', &c., and to obviate a breach of it, the final letter must in each case be considered as accompanied by the sign تشديد t'shdīd, making these words equivalent to adda, padda, makka, appa, d'rri, agamma, s'galla, atamma, sukka, dukka and chitta, respectively. Modern practice has removed the dfficulty with regard to some of them, by making them conform to the general practice, and placing a حرف مد huruf madd in the

penultimate, thus it is more common now to find
دوك , سوك , اتام , اكُم and چيت , but *d'rri*,
when alone, is less correctly written درى and the remainder have not been changed. We have seen that the
Malays rarely use the تشديد *t'shdīd*, and it is in fact a
refinement hardly applicable to Malay, but if the rule be not
accepted, then it must follow that a short open syllable may
have the accent, as in سده *sūdah* 'finished', جكلو *ji-*
kálaw ' if', سگل *s'gála* ' all ', which seems an impossibi-
lity, but all difficulty would be obviated by the employment of
تشديد *t'shdīd*, rendering the words equivalent to *sud-*
dah, jikallaw, and *s'galla.* Malays pay little attention to
such niceties of distinction, though they recognize that the
penultimate in such words cannot have a حرف *huruf*
madd. In the abbreviated forms of جكلو *jikalaw* viz.,
kalaw and *jika,* the former is, however, usually written with
an ١, كالو *ka-law,* but ى is not used in جك *jika,*
As a corollary to the rule stated at the beginning of the
Paragraph, might be added :—' there is no word in the language consisting only of *long* pure syllables' (compare Par. 46).
The only difficulty in the case of this rule would be where the
two long vowels are joined in a diphthong (compare Pars. 41
and 91), but it has been already observed that the words in
which this takes place are more in the nature of monosyllables.

SECTION XIV.

PREFIXED PARTICLES *

94. The prefixed particles may be thus arranged :—

CLASS 1.— م *m'* with its euphonic changes مغ *m'ng,* مڠ *m'ñ,* من *m'n,* and مم *m'm.* And ف *p'* with its changes ڤغ *p'ng,* ڤن *p'ñ,* ڤن *p'n,* and ڤم *p'm.*

CLASS 2.— ك *ka,* and س *sa* or *s'.*

CLASS 3.— د *di,* بر *b'r* بل *b'l* or ب *b',* تر *t'r* or ت *t',* ڤر *p'r* ڤل *p'l* or ف *p',* ك or كو *ku,* and كو *kaw.*

CLASS 4.— ال *'l, ul, il,* or *al.*

95. From the number of changes, which the particles م *m'* and ف *p'* undergo, according to the initial letter of the radical to which they are prefixed, and their effect upon such initial letter, they are the most important from an orthographical point of view. Though appearing somewhat complex, these changes in reality present little difficulty, for, as soon as the ear is accustomed to the Malay sounds, the tongue forms most of the derivatives correctly by natural selection.

96. The following are the rules which govern these changes, as formulated by FAVRE; they are based upon his Natural Alphabet of the language, as given in Tables VII and VIII above, to which the reader should refer. It must be remarked that the euphonic changes of these particles consist in the addition of the nasal letters.

---

* See note under Section XV. Par. 113.

RULE 1.—Take the nasal of the same class as the initial of the radical, and,

RULE 2.—If the initial letter of the radical be hard, delete it (but if soft, retain it).

RULE 3.—If the initial letter of the radical be a nasal, liquid, or semivowel, use the particles م *m'* and ڤ *p'*.

RULE 4.—When the radical commences with a vowel sound, or ه *h*, use the nasal غ *ng*.

RULE 5.—With the sibilant س *s*, take the nasal ڽ *ñ*, and delete س *s*.

N. B.—With the palatal class, the nasal ن *n* of the dental class is more commonly used than ڽ *ñ*, and in this case, the hard چ *ch* is preserved.

97. The application of these rules will be seen in the following examples :—

كات	*ka-ta* 'say'	مغات	*m'ng-a-ta.*
ڬرس	*ga-ris* 'scratch'	مڠݢارس	*m'ng-ga-ris.*
غارڠ	*nga-rung* 'grumble'	مغارڠ	*m'-nga-rung.*
چهاري	*ch'ha-ri* 'seek'	منچهاري	*m'n-ch'ha-ri.*
جاݢ	*ja-ga* 'watch'	منجاݢ	*m'n-ja-ga.*
پال	*ña-la* 'flame'	مپال	*m'ña-la.*
تاره	*ta-roh* 'place'	مناره	*m'na-roh.*
دڠر	*dengar* 'listen'	مندڠر	*m'n-dengar.*
ننتي	*nanti* 'wait'	مننتي	*m'nanti.*
ڤوكل	*pu-kul* 'beat'	مموكل	*m'mu-kul.*
بورو	*bu-ru* 'hunt'	ممبورو	*m'm-bu-ru.*

مأسق	ma-sok ' enter '	—	عماسق	m'ma-sok.
راب	ra-ba ' feel '		مراب	m'ra-ba.
لاري	la-ri ' run '		ملاري	m'la-ri.
ورت	w'rta ' news '	—	مورت	m'w'rta.
أتكت	angkat ' lift '		متعتكت	m'ng-angkat.
ادو	a-du ' complain '		معادو	m'ng-a-du.
أيكت	i-kut ' follow '		متتكيكت	m'ng-i-kut.
أوڤه	u-pah ' wages '		معتوڤه	m'ng-u-pah.
هيلر	hi-lir ' flow '	—	متهيلر	m'ng-hi-lir.
سثك	sangka ' imagine '		ميثك	m'ñangka.
ساكت	sa-kit ' sick '		مياكت	m'ña-kit.

98. These illustrations are equally applicable to the particle ڤ *p'*. Exceptions to these rules will be found, but even in such cases, it is usually not incorrect to form the derivative in accordance with them, or, either the words will be found to be of foreign origin, or to have undergone some change in the Malay itself, thus :— ممڤياءي *m'm-puña-i* 'to own' from ڤوڠ *pu-ña* 'own', the latter is a contraction of امڤوڠ *ampu-ña*, of which the derivative, according to the above rules, would be متتمڤياءي *m'ng-ampuña-i*, containing three nasal sounds in the first part of the word, and the deletion of that of a different class seems to follow naturally. Further exceptions consist of, (1) the retention of the hard initial of the radical, (2) the deletion of the soft initial of the radical, (3) the employment of the nasal ڠ *ng* before

و *w*. The latter is explained by the و *w* at times in foreign words, partaking of the nature of an aspirate, as in the English ' which '.

99. The following is a further explanation of the employment of these particles :—

من *m'n* may precede words' with the initials ج *j*, چ *ch*, and د *d*, as in منچامو *m'n-ja-mu* 'to feast' منچابت *m'n-cha-but* 'to pluck out', مندیده *m'n-di-deh* 'to boil'. It sometimes precedes ت *t*, as in منتیته *m'n-ti-tah* 'to order'.

مغ *m'ng* is used before a vowel sound, an aspirate, and the letter ک *g*, as in مغاجر *m'ng-a-j'r* 'to teach', مغاوفه *m'ng-u-pah* 'to hire', مغهمپیری *m'ng-hampi-ri* 'to approach, مغحضرکن *m'ng-ḥadl'r-kan* 'to make ready', مغغناپي *m'ng-g'na-pi* 'to complete'. The ا initial should be omitted in all cases, except when it should, in the radical, bear the مد *maddah*, and its elision is better marked by ء · مغنتق *m'ng-antok* 'to doze, sleep ', مغیدر *m'ng-i-dar* 'to revolve', but if the ا should properly bear the mark in the radical, this mark is, according to Malay custom, omitted, but the ا is retained, and it would seem more correct that it should be preceded by ء , and so from اکو *a-ku* 'I' is formed مغاکو *m'ng-a-ku* 'to acknowledge'. We shall see later that, by the application of suffixed particles, the initial ا may lose its مد *maddah*, and the suffixed particle having removed one half of the duplication indicated by this mark, the prefixed particle disposes of the remainder, leaving only ء in its place, hence we find ڤغاکوءن *p'ng-aku-an* ' acknowledgment'.

The principle of this has been before explained (Pars. 81-3). Malays frequently omit also the ه initial, and mark its elision by ء , but this seems less correct, thus from هابس *ha-bis* is formed معڠابس *m'ng-a-bis* ' to finish' (*see* Appendix A).

مم *m'm* precedes the letter ب *b* as in ممبایر *m'm-ba-y'r* ' to pay', ممبونه *m'm-bu-noh* ' to kill', and sometimes though more rarely ف *p*, as in ممڤیله *m'm-pi-leh* ' to choose'. This is the form of the particle which is used when the radical has already received the prefix ڤر *p'r.*

ڤاتك ماسق مڠادف كباوه دولي ممڤرسمبهكن حال ایت
pa-tek ma-sok m'ng-a-dap ka-ba-wah du-li m'm-p'r-s'mbah-kan hal i-tu ' I come to your Majesty's feet and respectfully communicate the circumstance'.

م *m'* precedes the letters ر *r*, ل *l*, م *m*, ن *n*, و *w*, and ڽ *ñ*, as in موروسق *m'ro-sak* ' to break, spoil', ملنتس *m'lintas* ' to pass through', ممتیكن *m'mati-kan* ' to put an end to', مننتي *m'nanti* ' to wait', موورتاكن *m'w'rta-kan* ' to publish', and مڽاڽي *m'ña-ñi* ' to sing'. It sometimes occurs before the soft aspirate ه , as in مهیل *m'he-la* ' to draw, drag'. مڠالووركن *m'ng-alu-war-kan* ' to turn out' is no exception, for it is not immediately formed from the radical اور *lu-war* ' outside', but from its derivative كلور *kalu-war* ' to the outside', the initial ك *k* being, as we have seen, dropped on the application of مڠ *m'ng.*

100. When the initial of the radical is ت *t*, that letter is dropped, and من *m'n* is used, the ن *n* taking the

vowel sound of the deleted letter of the radical, thus from
تولغ *to-long* is formed منولغ *m'no-long* 'to aid', from
تورت *tu-rut* منورت *m'nu-rut* 'to follow', from ترجن
t'rjun منرجن *m'n'rjun* 'to leap down', from تڠكس *tang-kis* منڠكس *m'nang-kis* 'to parry, ward off'.

When the initial of the radical is س *s*, that letter is
dropped, and مڽ *m'ñ* is used, the ن *ñ* taking the vowel
sound of the deleted letter of the radical, thus from سمڤي
sampay is formed ميمڤي *m'ñampay* 'to arrive', from
سوروه *su-roh*, ميڽوروه *m'ñu-roh* 'to order'. This modification sometimes occurs with ج *j* and چ *ch*, but less
correctly, as in ڤيوچق *p'ñu-chok* 'a fork', from چوچق
chu-chok 'to prod, pierce'. A derivative already formed
with the particle س *s'* is subject to a similar change, thus
from روف *ru-pa* 'form, appearance', سروف *s'ru-pa* 'alike'
(lit. 'one form') is obtained, ميڽروفاكن *m'ñ'rupa-kan* 'to render alike'.

When the initial of the radical is ك *k*, that letter is
dropped, and ڠ *ñ'ng* is used, as in مڠڽڤس *m'ng-i-pas*
'to fan', from كيڤس *ki-pas* 'fan'. We have already explained why the marking of the deletion of ك *k* by ء is
recommended. It is used for this purpose by the translators
of the Bible, but is said not to occur in any recognized native
composition. The ء is, however, found in some old writings
in a sense analogous, namely, the insertion of a vowel sound
after this particle, as مڠعتهوي *m'ng-'-tahu-i* 'to know',
ڤڠعتهوان *p'ng-'-tahu-an* 'knowledge'. (*See* Appendices).

101. The elision of ک *k* from the radical sometimes occasions a curious ambiguity in a derivative, by making it assume the identical form of another derivative, the initial of which is ا ; thus, from كارغ *ka-rang* 'to compose, indite', and ارغ *a-rang* 'charcoal', the derivative, ثغارغ *p'ng-a-rang* may mean either 'the author of a book', or 'a charcoal maker'.

102. There only now remain to be noticed the letters expressing a foreign element. The Malays have a tendency to assimilate such letters to the sounds of their own language, and to apply the particles in the same, according to the sound to which such foreign sound is assimilated, and hence when different persons apply different values to these foreign letters, the result may be that they apply different forms of the particles. Approximately the particles are applied as follows:— ث being pronounced like *s* forms ڽ *ñ*, as in ميابتکن *m'ña-bit-kan* 'to prove, substantiate', but منثابتکن *m'n-thsa-bit-kan* is met with. ح *ḥ* being an aspirate takes مغ *m'ng*, as مثحكمكن *m'ng-ḥukum-kan* 'to sentence'. خ *kh* takes من *m'n*, as ملخننکن *m'n-khatan-kan* 'to circumcise,' but مخبركن *m'khabar* 'to recount' is met with. ذ *dz* and ز *z* take من *m'n*. ش *sh* is sometimes changed to ڽ *ñ*, as in ميهيدکن *m'ñahid-kan* 'to bear witness, publish', but منشرطكن *m'n-sharat-kan* 'to reduce to rule, or law' is met with. ص *s* ض *dl* ط *t* and ظ *tl* take من *m'n*. ع *ain* and غ *ghr* take مغ *m'ng*. ف *f* takes مم *m'm*. And ق *k* takes مغ *m'ng*.

چڠتهوٴي دان ٿغَنُل دغن ٿُغَنَهُوٴن دان ٿغَنُل يڠ سمٿرن

m'ng-tahu-i dan m'ng-'nal d'ngan p'ng-tahu-an dan p'ng-'nal yang s'mporna ' to know and remember with perfect knowledge and recollection '.

103. There are a number of Malay words, really derivatives, but of which the radicals have been lost, notable among them are ماكن *ma-kan* ' to eat ', and ماتي *ma-ti* ' die ', from the Javanese ٿاكن *pa-kan* ' food ', and ٿاتي *pa-ti* ' death '. In forming derivatives from them there is no exception to rule.

104. The particles كـ *ka*, and س *sa* or *s'*, cause no change in the orthography of the word to which they are prefixed, except the elision of أ *alif* برٴبارس *b'r-ba-ris*, and its replacement by ء, as already noticed (Par. 62); but if ا should properly bear the mark ٓ, that mark is lost in the derivative, but a ء is employed before the ا. We have already remarked (Par. 99), that the ا of the radical may lose its ٓ, by the application of a suffixed particle (*and see* Par. 115 etc., below), in which case it remains برٴبارس *b'r-ba-ris*, and is liable to be deleted by the application of these particles.

105. According to modern usage the particles د *di* بر *b'r*, بل *b'l*, تر *t'r*, ٿر *p'r*, ٿل *p'l*, كـ or كو *ku*, and *kaw*, cause no change in the orthography of the word to which they are prefixed, but in some older writings they are found to cause similar changes to those noticed in the case of كـ *ka* and س *sa* or *s'*.

106. ال *al* is the Arabic definite article. It is joined to the word it precedes, but is only used in Arabic phrases, and, in general, causes no change in the orthography of the word to which it is prefixed. When two nouns are joined by the sign وصله, *waslah* ـ being applied to the ا of this particle, we have seen that the ا is rendered mute, and the final vowel of the first word unites with the ل of the particle.

ex. : شَرِيفُ الأَصل *shari-ful as'l* 'noble race, or lineage'. Which vowel this should be, depends upon the case of the first noun, and if nominative it is ´ *u*, if genitive ِ *i*, and if accusative ´ *a*, thus :—

Nom. امِيرُالمُؤمِنِين *ami-rul-mu-mini-na* 'Commander of the Faithful'.

Gen. امِيرِالمُؤمِنِين *ami-ril-mu-mini-na* 'of the Commander of the Faithful'.

Acc. امِيرَالمُؤمِنِين *ami-ral-mu-mini-na* 'Commander of the Faithful'.

This will explain also why the name عبدالله is pronounced *Abdullah* meaning 'Servant of God'. Further, if the initial of the second noun be a solar letter, the sound of the ل *l* is also lost, and the solar letter is doubled ; as in كتاب النبي *kita-bunnabi* 'book of the prophet'. It is a general rule in Arabic Orthography, that, when a letter is rejected for the sake of an abbreviation, the following letter receives a تسديد *t'shdīd*, and some writers have applied this rule to the prefixes in Malay (*see* Appendices). Some remarks upon the particle ال *al* will be found in Pars. 58 and 59, but if the reader

desires further information, he must consult an Arabic
grammar.

107. The word يڠ *yang* 'which, who, the', is often
joined to a word following it, and occasionally to one preceding it, but it causes no change in the orthography. The practice is mere capricious license of the pen, and this word
cannot be considered as a particle. The words دان *dan*
'and' and لَڬِي *la-gi* 'more', when occurring together, are
also commonly joined, دانلَڬِي .

108. The particles بر *b'r*, تر *t'r*, and فُر *p'r*,
sometimes drop the ر *r* (*see* Appendices), but no rule can
be laid down; the deletion seems optional, except when the
initial of the word is ر *r*, or is immediately followed by that
letter. The omission occurs much more frequently in speaking than in writing. The commonest instances are before
the letters س *s*, ث *p*, and ل *l*, ex. gr., دڤسرتكن
di-p'-s'rta-kan 'accompanied by', فلياَرن *p'laya-ran* 'voyage',
بڤرڠ *b'p'rang* or برڤرڠ *b'r-p'rang* 'to fight', and when two of
these particles are prefixed, the first drops the ر *r*, as in
بڤرسمبهكن خبر *b'-p'r-sambah-kan khabar* 'to communicate
intelligence', تڤرالس *t'-p'r-a-las* 'founded'.

109. The instances in which بر *b'r* and فُر *p'r*, exchange the ر *r* for ل *l* are very rare. Examples:—
بلاجر *b'l-a-j'r* 'to receive instruction', فلاجارن *p'l-aja-ran*
'school' فلبهاڬِي *p'l-b'ha-gi* 'division' (but with this radical, if the particle be بر *b'r*, the change does not take
place برباهاڬِي *b'r-b'ha-gi* 'to be divided'). بلانتار *b'lanta-ra*
'a waste, desert, trackless forest'.

110. In the study of Malay, the student may find some difficulty with regard to two of the prefixed particles. As shown above, there are two particles which begin with the letter ف *p*, and each undergoes euphonic modifications, the one ف *p'*, ڤع *p'ng*, ڤى *p'ñ*, ڤن *p'n*, or ڤم *p'm*, and the other ڤر *p'r*, ڤل *p'l*, or ف *p'*. Now the meanings of these particles are widely different, but in one of their modifications, ف *p'*, their forms may coincide, and they are at first difficult to distinguish. As, therefore, the correct spelling depends upon the meaning, an explanation of the latter will not be out of place, but will be mainly limited to the only instance in which it would be pardonable that confusion should occur, viz., in derivative *nouns*. To distinguish the particles they will be called ڤع *p'ng*, and ڤر *p'r*. (*See* Appendix B).

111. ڤر *p'r*, in general, marks the subject of the action expressed by the radical word, or, the receipt of such action or, the place of such action, whilst ڤع *p'ng* gives the agent by whom the action is performed, the instrument used, or the faculty, the former partaking of a neuter, or passive, and the latter, of an active signification; and corresponding to nouns formed from a verb in English, by adding 'or' 'er', as 'con·signor', 'seller', &c., as the former (with ڤر) do to similar nouns, formed by adding ' ee ', as ' consignee', 'bailee'. If, in addition to the prefix, the derivative take the suffix ن، *an*, then a noun is formed, analogous to a participial noun in English, in the case of ڤر *p'r*, corresponding to that formed from the past participle, as ' the taught ', and in the case of

فغ *p'ng*, from the present participle, as 'the teaching',
Thus, from اجر *a-j'r* is formed مغڠاجر *m'ng-a-j'r* 'to teach'
براجر *b'r-a-j'r*, or بلاجر *b'l-a-j'r* 'to receive instruction'
(hence often translated 'to learn'), ڤغاجر *p'ng-a-j'r* 'the
teacher', ڤلاجر *p'l-a-j'r* 'the pupil, recipient of instruction ',
ڤغاجرن *p'ng-aja-ran* 'the teaching', ڤلاجرن *p'l-aja-ran*
'the taught (matter), the subject of instruction', and, as we
have seen, 'the place of the action, school'. And so, from
بونه *bu-noh* 'to kill', ڤمبونه *p'm-bu-noh* 'a murderer',
ڤربونوهن *p'r-buno-han* 'the killed'. From بورو *bu-ru* 'to
hunt' ڤمبورو *p'm-bu-ru* 'hunter', ڤمبروءن *p'm-buru-an* 'the
hunting', ڤربروءن *p'r-buru-an* 'the hunted, the game, the field'
ادا که ڤد تمڤت اين ڤرسڠݢاهن باݢي اورغ يغ برالله ڤد ڤرجلاننڽ
ada-kah pada t'mpat i-ni p'r-singga-han ba-gi o-rang yang
b'r-l'lah pada p'r-jala-nan-ña 'Is there, in this place, *a*
place of call for those who are weary on their *way?'*

112. In those cases in which the forms of the particles
coincide, the student must examine the initial of the radical,
and, if it would have undergone change had the particle
فغ *p'ng* been used, but has not done so, then he will know
that the other particle is employed. Thus ڤڤراغن *p'-p'ra-*
ngan is 'the field of battle', but ڤمراغن *p'm'ra-ngan* is 'the
battle, the fighting'. And so, ڤسروهن *p'-suro-han* is 'the
ordered', but ڤڽروهن *p'ñuro-han* is 'the ordering'. The
reader is again cautioned, that these remarks apply only
to derivative *nouns*, for ڤر *p'r* also marks one of the
phases of the verb, whilst فغ *p'ng* always indicates a
noun, and further, that these derivatives are by no means

regular in their formation, but show many exceptions mostly depending upon certain peculiarities in the meaning conveyed by the radical word. It may perhaps assist the reader to trace the meanings of these derivatives to explain that the particle ﻓﺮ *p'r* is in all probability taken from the Sanscrit *pra* (Latin *pro*. French *pour*) and can often be rendered in English by ' for ', and hence, ﻓﺮﺑﺮﻭﻥ *p'r-buru-an* is ' a thing, or place, *for* hunting ', ﻓﭙﺮﺍﻏﻦ *p'-p'ra-ngan* ' a place *for fighting* ' ﻓﺮﺍﺩﻭﻥ *p'r-adu-an* ' a place *for repose* ', ﻓﺮﺍﺭﺍﻛﻦ *p'r-ara-kan* ' a thing *for procession*, a triumphal car '. The same meaning of this particle is traceable through most of the derivatives verbs formed with it. If, in these cases, the radical word itself describes an act, the employment to the particle mostly indicates, that the action does not proceed immediately from the agent, but through, or by, some other agent, or means, not named, thus from ﻫﻤﻔﻦ *himpun* ' to assemble ' is formed ﻣﻤﻔﺮﻫﻤﻔﻨﻜﻦ *m'm-p'r-himpun-kan* ' to cause to assemble (by messengers)'. But if the radical word describes an object, then the derivative verb usually means to do some act, not expressed, or render in a certain state, through, by, or by means of, that object, as ﻣﻤﻔﺮﺍﻧﻘﻜﻦ *m'm-p'r-a-nak-kan* ' to beget, to cause to be with child, or bear '. And so, from ﺳﻤﺒﻪ *sambah* which means either ' an obeisance ' or ' to make obeisance ' is formed ﻓﺮﺳﻤﺒﻪﻛﻦ *p'r-sambah-kan* meaning ' to do some act (not expressed) respectfully, or with formal courtesies ' and hence it may mean ' to present, tell, offer, or receive &c.' ' to submit '.

SECTION XV.

SUFFIXED PARTICLES.

113. It must be borne in mind that the tendency in the language is to place the accent on the penultimate syllable, whether in the radical, or in the derivative word, and, if the penultimate be an open syllable, the حرف مد *ḥurúf madd*, or letter of prolongation of sound, will generally be found there. If, however, in derivative words, the penultimate, or any intermediate syllable, be closed, the long vowel will mostly be found in the open syllable (if any) immediately preceding such closed syllable.

NOTE.—Though prefixed and suffixed particles are freely added to words taken from the Arabic, it is not usual to alter the orthography of the Arabic word in consequence of the application of the particles. Except in the particulars from time to time noted (as in Pars. 29 and 102), it may be taken that such word undergoes no change by their application. The suffixes ءن *an* and ءي *i*, however, would render open a closed ultimate syllable, as حکم *ḥukam* حکمن *ḥukuman* ' sentence, decree '.

114. The suffixed particles may be thus arranged :—

CLASS 1.—ءن *an* and ءي *i* or ِ *i*.

CLASS 2.—کن *kan*. ت or کو *ku*. ِم or مو *mu*, ن *ûn*, ل *lah*, ک *kah*, and ة *tah*.

CLASS 3.—ءند *'nda*, or ءندد *'ndah*.

115. With regard to ءن *an*, and ءي *i*, if the ultimate syllable of the radical be closed, the application of these particles renders it open, and gives it a حرف مد *ḥurúf*

madd, homogeneous with the vowel sign of the first letter of the syllable, the closing letter of the syllable loses its جزم *jazm,* and is carried on to the particle, forming with it a distinct syllable. Thus from كُنف *g'nap* ' whole ' is formed مغُكنافي *m'ng-g'na-pi* ' to complete ', from تغكغ *tunggang* ' to straddle, sit astride ', تغكاغن *tungga-ngan* ' that which is astride ' سكل توغكاغن كودا دان كلدي *s'gala tungga-ngan* (تغكاغن) correct) *ku-da dan kaldai* ' all the horsemen and riders of asses ' (lit. ' all those astride of horses and asses '). If the penultimate of the radical be long, it becomes short, and if it have a حرف مد *huruf madd,* the same is omitted ; thus, from ماكن *ma-kan* ' to eat ', is formed مكانن *maka-nan* ' victuals '; from تولس *tu-lis* ' write, delineate ', تليسن *tuli-san* ' things delineated, written, drawn ', from ڤاكي *pa-kay* ' to use ', ڤاكاين *paka-yan* ' clothes, things worn, or used '; from جالن *ja-lan* ' to move, proceed', منجلاني *m'n-jala-ni* ' to perambulate ', يغ كوجلاني اتس *yang ku jala-ni a-tas-ña* ' whereon I have walked ' (*parcouru*), from دوري *du-ri* ' a thorn ' درين *duri-an* ' thorny, the fruit of this name ', ڤوهن بوه سڤرت دران دان رمبوتن *po-hun bu-wah bu-wah s'p'rti duri-an dan rambu-tan* ' fruit trees such as durian and rambutan (lit. thorny fruit and hairy fruit)'. By the operation of this rule, an initial ا bearing the mark ~ مد *maddah,* loses that mark in the derivative, and from أجر *a-j'r* ' teach ' is formed أجاري *aja-ri* ; and from أتر *a-tur* ' to arrange ', أتورن *atu-ran* ' arrangement '. It has already been explained (Pars. 55 and 56) how these particles

affect a word, having a weak letter marked with تشديد
t'shdîd, that mark being lost in the derivative word, thus
from ديم di-yam ' to dwell, remain, stay quiet ' equivalent
to تمشت كديامن مانسي, ديم is formed كديامن ka-diya-man,
t'mpat ka-diya-man ma-nusiya ' a place of human habitation '.
If the ultimate syllable of the radical be open, it should take a
حرف مد ḥuruf madd homogeneous with its vowel sign, followed by the mark ء . Thus from كات ka-ta ' to say ', is
formed مغتاءي m'ng-ata-i ' to tell ', and فركتاءن p'r-kata-an
' words, speech '; from لاك or لاكو la-ku ' action ',
ملكوءي m'laku-i ' to cause to happen ', and كلكوءن ka-
laku-an ' behaviour '; from فوج or فوجي pu-ji ' praise '
كفجيءن ka-puji-an ' praises, compliments '.

116. It would appear, that in the case of كسره k'srah
or ضمه dlammah final, the همزه hamzah might be re-
placed by the mark تشديد t'shdîd, and the last mentioned
two words might be written كلكون ka-laku-wan, and
كفجين ka-puji-yan. This practice is little followed by
the Malays, but it seems to have been recognized in some
words, such as, كمدين k'mdi-yan ' then, after ' سكلين
s'k'li-yan ' all ' هلون halu-wan ' bow, or prow ' and دمكين
d'm'ki-yan ' such, so,' in which the ء is nearly always
omitted. The use of an ا after و as mentioned in the note
to Par. 55 is much more common.

117. In radicals of which the ultimate syllable is a diphthong, and which, for the purposes of this work, has been
treated as a closed syllable, the same should follow the rule
above laid down as to closed syllables, and ڤاكي pa-kay

'to use', become ڤكاين *paka-yan* 'clothes, things used';
كيلو *ki-law* 'shining', كلاون *kila-wan* brightness'. This
is, however, not strictly followed by the Malays, and one
often finds such spellings as كيلوءن and كلوان *kilaw-an*
&c., even in the best writings.

118. Those words containing a diphthong, but consisting
of four letters, the first and final being strong letters, and the
2nd and 3rd weak letters, seem, as has been noticed (Par. 92),
to undergo no other change, than the carrying of the final
letter on to the particle.

N. B.—It must be remembered that there is this difference
between ءن *an*, and ءي *i*, that the former is a closed
syllable, and acts as a stop, and the addition of subsequent particles, makes no further change in the orthography
of the derivative word to that point, or of the particle
itself; ex. gr. ڤركتاءنمولـه *p'r-kata-an-mu-lah* 'your words',
but that ءي *i*, being open, will, if followed by another
particle, itself become the accented syllable, and lose its
effect upon the ultimate of the radical, so far as the giving it a
حرف مد *ḥuruf madd* is concerned. Thus, from كيرم
ki-rim 'send', is formed مڠيريمي *m'ng-iri-mi* 'to send'
دكيريمـڽ *di-kirimi-ña* 'there was sent by him', and from
كات *ka-ta* 'say', مڠاتاءي *m'ng-ata-i*, دكتاءيلـه *di-kataï-
lah* 'there was said'. It must also be borne in mind
that, though the letter ي is usually written when the
particle ءي is employed, it is so, in accordance with
common practice referred to in Par. 46 above, but would
appear to be more correctly represented by the sign كسره

k'srah placed under the final letter, if that letter be employed
as a consonant, or under the ‌ه‌ , if the final vowel has become prolonged by حرف مد‌ ḥuruf madd, and so, it would
seem more correct to write مغذُريمي‌ than مغذُريمي‌ , and كتاء‌
than كتاءي‌ , for in these cases it does not appear necessary
that the final vowel sound should be prolonged by حرف مد‌
ḥuruf madd.

119. There is one more change to be noted as caused by
these two particles, viz., that following a syllable closed by
ق‌ k, this letter is exchanged for ك‌ , thus from كوتق‌
ko-tok 'curse' is formed ككوتوكن‌ ka-koto-kan 'curse' (passive), and مغذُتوكي‌ m'ng-oto-ki 'to curse'. There seems
no reason for this change, unless upon the supposition
that ك‌ k is a definite sound with the Malays, whilst ق‌
k final, as used in the primitive words, is indefinite, and often
nearly silent and, in that state, unfit to receive a vowel, but
the practice is universal. It certainly tends to raise a difficulty for the student, in discriminating between the particles
ءن‌ an and كن‌ kan, and it is very common in Malay
writing to find such words as ka-baña-kan written كباپقكن‌
instead of كبپكن‌ showing that the Malays themselves find a
difficulty in distinguishing these two particles, and often render their sentences ungrammatical by such mistakes, for the
meanings are widely different : ex. gr., ڤرانكن‌ p'r-ana-
kan means 'the womb; the offspring, race, the begotten',
but ڤرانقكن‌ p'r-a-nak-kan, 'to engender, beget, begotten'
and ڤراراكن‌ p'r-ara-kan means 'procession', but ڤرارقكن‌
p'r-arak-kan 'form or carry in procession'. Similar

mistakes are often made with the particle ـي , and one often finds مـمـبـايـكي m'm-bay-ki 'to repair, make good' written مـمـبـايـقـكي m'm-bayk-ki, which would be meaningless, for there is no so such particle as كي ki.

120. With regard to the particles كن kan, ك or كو ku abbreviation of اكو a-ku 'I, me, mine', م or مو mu abbreviation of كامو ka-mu 'thou, thee, thine, you, ye your', ڽ ña 'he, him, his, she, her, they, them, their', له lah (expletive), كه kah and ته tah (interrogative), if the ultimate syllable of the radical or derivative word be closed, these particles cause no change of orthography, but if such syllable be open, but be preceded by a closed syllable, it must take a حرف مد ḥuruf ma kl. So far, the rules are simple, and lead to a spelling consistent with the ordinary practice of Malay writers, but when we come to deal with the effect of the application of these particles to radical words, having both the ultimate and penultimate syllables open, some little difficulty occurs. The rule which has met with most approval by European writers, and it is easy to quote from Malay writings in support of it, would seem to be, that the ultimate should take a حرف مد ḥuruf madd and the penultimate become short and lose its حرف مد ḥuruf m dd (if any), and, if consisting of ا , lose the mark ٓ . The following are examples of derivatives formed in accordance with the above rules:—from اڠكت aṇgkat 'lift', اڠكتكن aṇgkat-kan 'cause to be lifted'; from انق a-nak 'child' انقك or انقكو a-nak-ku 'my child', انقم or انقمو a-nak-mu 'your child', انقڽ a-nak-ña 'his or their child'; from ايكت

i-kut 'follow, accompany', ايكتله *i-kut-lah* 'follow', ايكتكه *i-kut-kah* or ايكتته *i-kut-tah* 'follow ?' : from فنت *pinta* request, ask for', فنتاكن *pinta-kan* 'to ask for', فنتاك or فنتاكو *pinta-ku* 'my request', فنتامو or فنتام *pinta-mu* 'your request', فنتان *pinta-ña* 'their or his request' فنتاكه *pinta-kah* 'is it a request ?', 'is it asked for ?' : from كات *ka-ta* 'say', كتاكن *kata-kan* 'to say, give out'; from جادي *ja-di* 'become' جديكن *jadi-kan* 'to create, cause to be'; from كيچو *ki-chu* 'to cheat' كيچوك* or كيچوكو* *kichu-ku* 'my fraud', كيچون* *kichu-ña* 'his or their fraud' كيچوكه* *kichu-kah* 'is it fraud ?' The application of the rule appears, however, to lead to results, in the latter instances, which are not quite satisfactory, and which are so much at variance with the practice of the Malay writers, that it seems necessary, that the rule should be in some way modified. But considering that the rule has been accepted and confirmed by almost every writer of authority on the language, it is with very great diffidence that a suggestion is offered, that this treatment of the radical words, having both penultimate and ultimate syllables open, even though supported by such an authority as MARSDEN, is questionable ; some instances of such orthography may occur in native writings, but they seem to be more theoretic deductions than actual phonetic spellings of the words they represent. A more feasible deduction from a general study of Malay writing, and from the accent given by Malays to such derivatives, seems to be that, if the vowel sounds of both

---

* Questionable.

syllables are homogeneous, the accent is changed to the penultimate of the derivative word, as in كتأڽ *kata-ña* 'he said', چوچون *chuchu-ña* 'her grandson', درين *diri-ña* 'herself', but that, if the vowels are heterogenous, the radical preserves the حرف مد *huruf madd* in the penultimate, unless the sound be that of the vowel فتح *fat-hah*. It is true, however, that the weak letter in the ultimate of the radical is commonly inserted upon the principle stated in Par. 46, but it would seem that this spelling is conventional, and that the weak letter, in the ultimate of the radical, should, notwithstanding the suffix, be still considered as a substitute only for the vowel sign, and not حرف مد *huruf madd*. In the following examples the vowels are homogeneous بارغ ڤركتأءن يغدبچاڽ ايت *ba-rang p'r-kata-an yang di-bacha-ña i-tu* 'whatever words were so read by them', منثر كات چچوڽ دمكين ايت *m'nengar ka-ta chuchu-ñ d'm'ki-yan i-tu* 'to hear her grandson so speak', كارن چهاي بولن ايت تياد چهاي درين *ka-rana ch'ha-ya bu-lan i-tu tiya-da ch'ha-ya diri-ñ* 'for the brightness of the moon is not her own brightness', سرت ممباو بنين *s'rta m'm-ba-wa bini-ña* 'bringing his wife with him' دأيهت ڤد سسيڽ اد سؤرغ ڤرمڤوان دودق *di-li-hat pada sisi-ñ ada s'o-rang p'r-ampu-an du-duk* 'he saw by his side (there was) a woman sitting'. But in one phrase we find كتأڽ *kata-ña* and گوننن *gu-naña*, and in another رجأڽ *raja-ña* and روڤان *ru-pa-ñ*, these seem to show that a distinction should be made in the case of heterogeneous vowels, and it would appear more correct not to employ the weak letter in the

penultimate of the derivative, but to write *ru-pañ.ı* روٴپٔن .
Several educated Malays, who were consulted as to these
words, held that the accent should not change in such words
as the latter. It is apparently upon this principle that,
throughout one entire book, we find the derivatives of
اين *i-ni* 'this', and ايت *i-tu* 'that', written انيله *ini-lah*
and ايتوله (ايتله) *i-'u-lah*. We would therefore suggest that
the student will, by preserving the orthography of the radical,
unless the vowels be homogeneous, or the vowel sound in
the penultimate be that of فتحه *fat-ḥah*, more nearly
conform to the practice of the better native writers in the use
of these particles, but the books are so irregular, that it is
impossible to lay down from them any definite rule, and it
may well be doubted whether, if the ordinary colloquial
pronunciation be followed, which as often as not shows no
change of the accent, when particles of this class are applied,
the radicals should not always preserve their primitive
orthography. Or, if it be held that the accent changes in some,
but not in others, it may be that the vowels ضمه *ḍlammah*
and كسره *k'srah* have a greater tenacity than فتحه *fat-*
ḥah, and compel the latter to give way to them, but, as was
remarked earlier (Par. 15) the change of accent (if any) is
very slight. But there can be little doubt that the retention
of the حرف مد *ḥuruf madd* in the penultimate of the radical,
when derivatives are formed by the first class of particles
(ءن *au* and ءي *i*), is unjustifiable, though most Malay
writings contain instances of it. The accent is the safest
guide, and with these particles it always changes; thus

فُتوسن *putu-san* is formed from فُوتس *pu-tus* ' to break off, cease', يڠتياد برفتوسن بارڠ سبنتر جوڬ *yang tiya-da b'r-putu-san ba-rang s'bant'r ju-ga* ' which did not cease even for a single instant ', and فتنتورن *p'-totu-ran* from توتر *to-tur* ' to speak, converse,' ملك ادڤون فتنتورنمو ايتوله جوڬ مننجقکن كڤرچيان مو ايت بوهوڠ اداڽ *maka ada-pun p'-totu-ran-mu i-tulah ju-ga m'nunjok-kan ka-p'r-chaya-an-mu i-tu bo-hong ada-ña* ' furthermore thy conversation also proveth, that wherein thou trusteth, to be false', درڤد ثرملاڽ سمڤي کسداهنڽ *d'ripada p'r-mula-an-ña sampay ka-suda-han-ña* ' from the beginning thereof even unto the end thereof', جكلاو کيت مللوءي تيته ايهندا *jikalau ki-ta m'lalu-i ti-tah ayahanda* ' if we exceed our august father's commands ', سڤاي بوله توانهمب مندافت کسناڠن سعمر هيدف *sopa-ya bu-leh' tu-wan-hamba m'n-da-pat ka-s'na-ngan s'-umur hi-dup* ' that my master may obtain comfort for his life long ', ڬنف بلاڠن سراتس کالي دراڽ ايت *g'nap bila-ngan s'ra-tus ka-li d'ra-ña i-tu* ' complete was the reckoning of the hundred blows of his castigation.'

121. کن *kan* has the same effect as عن *an* (Par. 118) in closing the derivative word, and the subsequent addition of particles causes no further change therein, but with regard to کو *ku*, مو *mu*, and ن *ña*, they, like ءي *i*, being open syllables, would seem to be liable, by the addition of subsequent particles, to lose their power to give a حرف مد *huruf madd* to the ultimate syllable of the radical, and they may in their turn become long, in which case they must carry a حرف مد *huruf madd*; thus, from انقک *a-nak-ku* ' my child ', انقكوله *a-nak-ku-lah* ' my child !'. As an instance of

three suffixed particles, where the first closes the derivative word, دكتاكنياله *di-kata-kan-ña-lah*. The particles له *lah*, که *kah*, and ته *tah*, are always ultimate.

122. From the foregoing the reader will remark, that the main exceptions to the general rule, as to the accent and حرف مد *huruf madd* being found in the penultimate syllable of a word, whether radical or derivative, are caused by the presence of closed syllables, and this should be borne in mind, throughout the comments upon the duplication of the radical, and compound words formed of two radicals.

123. عند *'nda* is a suffix applied in the courtly style to terms of relationship, &c. It is probably an abbreviation of اندا *inda'h* signifying 'rare, precious, uncommon', and this supposition is supported by the fact that these derivatives are often found written with a final ه *h* داتغله مغدف ايهنده بنده بكنده *da-tang-lah m'ng-n-dap ayahandah bondah bagindah* 'came into the presence of the royal father and mother'. Its application is sometimes governed by the same rules as the first class of suffixed particles, but in most cases a conventional spelling, with abbreviation, has grown up. Thus, from انق *a-nak* 'child' is formed انكنده *anakanda*, انقد *a-nak-da*, or انكده *anandah*, دبرين سوسو اكن انكند ايت *di-bri-ña su-su a-kan anak-anda i-tu* 'she gave her breast to the royal infant', انقد تغكل دغن يتيمث *anak-da tinggal d'ngan yatim-ña* 'the royal infant is left an orphan'. The term بند *bonda* 'mother' is a corruption of ايبو *i-bu* 'mother' and ند *'nda*. تياد مذاره ايهند دان بند *tiya-da m'na-roh ayahanda*

dan bonda ' not possessing father or mother ' (ایه *a-yah*
' father '). From ادق *a-dek* ' younger brother or sister ' is
formed ادندا *adinda*. From كاكق *ka-kak* ' elder brother,
or sister ' كڪندا *kakanda*. From مـدق *ma-mak* ' uncle,
or aunt ' ممندا *mamanda*. بڱند *baginda* ' His Highness '
is a corruption of بهڱي *b'hagīya* ' beatitude, majesty ', and
the same particle. سندا *sanda* ' I, we ,' appears to be formed
by the application of the same particle to سهاي *s'ha-ya* ' servant, slave ' (but used commonly as a pronoun of the first
person). This term, however, is essentially different in its
composition from the other instances given ; in them, the
particle is used as a sort of qualifying adjective to the word
to which it is annexed, but in سندا *sanda* the particle must
be taken to apply to the personage addressed, and not to the
speaker, and therefore, though ايهند *ayahanda* might be
translated ' August Father ' سندا *sanda* must be rendered
' slave of the august (person addressed) ', and not ' august
slave '.

124. It has not been thought necessary to treat the defining words اين *i-ni* ' this ' and ايت *i-tu* ' that ', as suffixed particles, though, if they follow a radical, the ultimate
syllable of which ends in فتّح *fat-hah* open, they are
usually joined to it, the only change which takes place is that
the ا is omitted, and its elision is marked by همزه *hamzah*, as راجئت *ra-ja-i-tu* ' that king ', راجئين *ra-ja-i-ni*
' this king ', مريكئت *marika-i-tu* ' they, those people '. يائت
ya-i-tu ' that is to say, that, that is ' appears, however, to be a
convention.

125. Similarly فون *pun* ' also' (but more frequently employed apparently as an expletive) is commonly joined to a word preceding it, but in no case is any change in the orthography of such word caused. As, ايتفون *i-tu-pun* ' thereupon', ملك هاريفون ثتغله *maka ha-ri-pun p'tang-lah* ' the night came on ' (lit. 'the day eveninged'), ملك كدوا مريكذيتفون دودقله *maka kadu-wa mari-ka-i-tu-pun da-duk-lah* 'the two of them sat down', ملك راجفون مغوچفله شوكر كفد الله *maka ra-ja-pun m'ng-u-chap-lah shu-kur kapada allah* ' and the king uttered his thanksgiving to God '. And so also, as has been already remarked (Par. 107), يڠ *yang* ' who, which' is sometimes joined to a word preceding it, as, اورڠيڠ *o-rang-yang* ' person who ', but the practice is mere license of the pen, and is not recommended.

SECTION XVI.

INTERPOSED PARTICLES.

126. These have no place in the ordinary Malay construction, but a few words in which they occur, are in common use. They are mostly taken, or imitated, from the Javanese, and must be considered as distinct words for orthographical purposes. They mainly consist of the interposition of a syllable, after the initial of the radical, by means of one of the letters ر *r*, ل *l*, or م *m*, which commonly takes the vowel belonging to the initial of the radical, and the accent, in accordance with the common practice of placing the latter on the penultimate syllable. In some instances the radicals have fallen into disuse, or only survive in a few districts. Examples of interposed particles:—تلاڤق *t'la-pak* from تاڤق *ta-pak* 'sole of the foot, or palm of the hand', تلنجق *t'lun-jok* 'the index, or fore finger', from تنجق *tunjok* 'to point out', كرنيت *k'r'nñut* 'to grind the teeth', from كنّت *k'n-ñut* 'grimace', كلنچر *g'linchir* 'to slip', from كنچر *ginchir* (not used), كمارو *k'ma-raw* 'the dry season' from كارو *ka-raw* 'second' (very rarely heard), كليلڠ *kuli-ling* 'around', from كولڠ *ku-ling* (not used, though ڬولڠ *gu-ling* 'to roll' is in common use), ڬمورة *g'mu-roh* 'roaring, resounding', from ڬورة *gu-roh* 'a deep sound'. And several instances occur in which both forms are used to give a sense of intensity, reciprocity, or frequency, as تورن تمورن *tu-run t'mu-run* 'descending (from generation to generation)', ڬيلڠ ڬميلڠ *gi-lang g'mi-lang* 'shining, flashing (to and fro)'.

It may not be out of place to notice here, that when اكو
a-ku ' I, we ', اڠكو angkaw ' you, thou ', and اي i-ya
' he, she, they ', follow a word ending in an open vowel, or a
nasal letter, the letter د d is often interposed for euphony,
forming داكو da-ku, ديكو di-kaw, and دي di-ya,
respectively. دتڠڬلكن داكو س‍يافكه ممليهراكنداكو ڤد هاري تواكو
di-tinggal-kan-ña da-ku si-apa-kah m'mlihara-kan (مملهراكن)
da-ku pada ha-ri tuwa-ku ' (if) I be deserted by him, who will
(there be to) cherish me in the days of my old age?'
دڤرجهاتيـڽ ديكو di-p'r-jahu-ti-ña di-kaw '(lest) thou be evilly
treated by them ', تنتو برجمڤڟله كيت دڠن دي t'ntu b'r-
jumpa-lah ki-ta d'ngan di-ya ' surely we shall meet with him '.
But the form دي di-ya is often used quite irrespectively
of what letter or vowel precedes it, and the particle ڽ ña
is but another euphonic change of the same pronoun. The
use of the latter form is, however, more idiomatic, and it
cannot in general be employed when it forms the subject
of the action of a transitive verb. It is invariably used in
the possessive, as رومهڽ ru-mah-ña ' his house ', نڬريڽ
n'gri-ña ' their country '; and in the peculiar impersonal,
or passive form of expression so common in Malay, as,
دڤلقڽ دان دچيمڽ di-p'lok-ña dan di-chi-yum-ña this would
generally be translated ' he embraced her and kissed her '
but would, however, be more accurately rendered ' then
kissed he , and embraced he '.

SECTION XVII.

DUPLICATION OF WORDS.

127. The duplication of the radical is most often indicated by the mark اڠكت *angka* ۲ , as already noticed, ex. gr., كادڠ ۲ *ka-dang ka-dang* ' sometimes '. Though such words may be, and often are, written at length and joined, as كادڠكادڠ , yet it seems preferable, in all cases in which they, if doubled, have the same orthography and pronunciation, to indicate the duplication by ۲ , but, whenever the orthography and accent should change, to write them at length and joined. Malays appear to write them according to caprice, but with a marked preference for the use of ۲ .

128. We shall proceed to consider how :—

  Firstly, the isolated radical,

  Secondly, the radical with prefix,

  Thirdly, the radical with suffix,

is dealt with.

129. If both the syllables of the isolated radical are open, each long syllable (if any) becomes short, and its vowel letter, or حرف مد *ḥuruf madd*, is dropped in the first part of the doubled word, whilst the second part preserves its orthography: thus, from لكي ۲ *la-ki* ' male ' is formed لكيلكي* *lakila-ki* ' husband, male ', from راج *ra-ja* ' king ', رجراج *rajara-ja* ' kings ', from ماتت *ma-ta* ' the eye ', متماتت *matama-ta* ' a constable, myrmidon '. It would seem that, if the ultimate syllable be open and long, as in سرو *s'ru* ' to call ', بري *b'ri*

---

* Questionable, but usual.

'give', pronunciation would require, that the long vowel be retained in the first part, and the duplication is therefore better indicated by ٢ as, ٢سرو s'ru-s'ru, ٢بري b'ri-b'ri. It would seem also that, upon the principle stated in the nòte to Par. 120, those words having heterogeneous vowels in the ultimate and penultimate syllables should be similarly treated, and that ٢كوډ ku-da ku-da would be more correct than كدكوډ kuduku-da, and ٢فوجي pu-ji pu-ji, than فجفوجي pujipu-ji.

130. If either of the syllables, of the isolated radical, and so much the more if both, be closed, the duplication should be indicated by ٢, ex. gr., ٢اورغ o-rang o-rang 'people', ٢فقس paksa paksa 'forces', ٢تڠكف tangkap tangkap 'catch'.

131. When both syllables of the radical are open, the duplication is sometimes formed by merely repeating the first letter, as ككورا k'ku-ra for ٢كورا or كوركور kuraku-ra 'tortoise', and ٢للاكي l'la-ki for ٢لكي or لكلاكي laki-la-ki 'husband, male'.

132. When the radical has a prefixed particle, the radical alone is repeated, and so, from بونه bu-noh 'to kill', is formed ٢ممبونه m'm-bu-noh-bu-noh, but if the initial letter of the radical is strong, and has disappeared by the applica-tion of a particle with a nasal sound (Pars. 96-7), this nasal is preserved in the duplication, and from كرغ ka-rang 'to set, compose, indite' is formed ٢مڠرغ or مڠرڠ٢رغ m'nga-rang nga-rang*, and from فوجي pu-ji 'praise' ٢مموجي

---

* This peculiarity supplies the principal argument against marking the elision of k in these words by hamzah. See Pars. 6 and 100 above, and Appendix A.

m'muji-mu-ji. A similar effect is apparently produced when such a particle is annexed to a radical, which both begins and ends with a vowel sound, and thus, from ايلو *e-lu* is formed مغنُّليلو or مغنَّيلو *m'nge-lu-nge-lu*, and from اد *ada* مغندَاد *m'ngada-ngada*, but where the radical begins with a vowel sound, but ends with حرف برجزم *huruf b'r-jazm*, the radical alone is repeated, and ر should be used, thus, from الر *a-lir* 'to flow' is formed مغالِر *m'ng-a-lir-a-lir*, and from اوگُت *u-gut* 'fear, terror', مغوگُت *m'ng-u-gut-u-gut.*

133. When the particle is to be prefixed to the second part, ر cannot be employed, and both parts of the duplicated word must be written at length, and it is better that they be not joined. Thus from كارغ *ka-rang* is formed كارغ مغارغ *ka-rang m'ng-a-rang*, and from تولغ *to-long* تولغ منلوغ *to-long m'no-long.* The following quotation contains a number of examples:— ستله تربت متهاري مك كليهاتنله اورغ برڤرغ ايت تراَلو امت رامين اوسر مغوسر دان ڤرغ ممرغ تمبق منمبق تيكم منيكم دان گوجه مغگوجه تمڤر منمڤر تندغ منندغ دان ڤالو ممالو سام ماتين كدواَن

s't'lah t'rbit mataha-ri maka ka-liha-tan-lah o-rang b'r-p'rang i-tu t'r-la-lu a-mat ra-may-ña u-sir m'ng-u-sir dan p'rang m'm'rang tumbuk m'numbuk ti-kam m'ni-kam dan gu-joh m'ng-gu-joh tamp'r m'namp'r t'ndang m'n'ndang dan pa-lu m'ma-lu sa-ma ma-ti-ña ka-duwa-ña ' when the sun rose, there were seen the men engaged in battle, in exceeding crowds, pursued and pursuing, attacked and attacking, struck and striking, slapped and slapping, kicked and kicking, beaten and beating, dying together, both parties '.

134. When the duplicated radical is followed by one or more
suffixed particles, the second part of the duplicated word should
be subject to change following the rules already laid down for
the application of suffixed particles, and, if the first suffixed
particle applied causes no change in the radical, and the
duplication of the radical is capable without the suffixed
particle of being expressed by ٢ , that form should be
preserved, and the particles placed after the ٢ , but where
the particle causes any change in the radical, then, though
without the particle, the duplication might be indicated by
٢ , as مُدَه٢ *mudah-mudah* 'very easily', yet with the
particle, this form should not be employed, but the whole
should be written at length, as مُدَهمُدَاهن *mudah-muda-han*
'perchance, perhaps it may be that'. The following are
further illustrations : —

اَنٿِ٢	*a-nak-a-nak.*
اَنٿِ٢ن	*a-nak-a-nak-ñ i.*
اَنٿِ اَناكن	*a-nak-ana-kan.*
ثَٿُݢَل٢	*panggil-panggil.*
دثَٿُݢَل٢ن	*di-panggil-panggil-ñ i.*
دثَٿُݢَلثَٿُݢَلِيلِي	*di-panggil-panggil-i.*
جَالن٢	*ja-lan-ja-lan.*
دجَالن٢ن	*di-ja-lan-ja-lan-ñ i.*
جَالنجَلانِي	*ja-lan-jala-ni.*

The more common practice is, however, to indicate these
duplications by ٢ , and to place the suffixed particles (if
any) after the figure.

SECTION XVIII.

UNION OF TWO RADICALS.

135. The rules to be observed in joining two radical words are nearly the same as those given for the duplication of words (saving the use of ر). The second word of such a combination preserves its orthography, unless changed by a suffixed particle. If both syllables of the first word are open, and the vowels are homogeneous, it should not retain a حرف مد *huruf madd* or long vowel, ex. gr., متهري *mataha-ri* 'the sun', from مات *ma-ta* 'the eye', هري *ha-ri* 'of day', هلبالغ *huluba-lang* 'a chieftain, commander', from هرلو *hu-lu* 'head', and بالغ *ba-lang* a corruption of بل *ba-la** 'people, soldiers', مهراج *mahara-ja* 'great king', from مه *maha* 'great (superlative)' and راج *ra-ja* 'king', مربهاي *marab'ha-ya* 'danger, evil, misfortune', from مار *ma-ra* and بهاي *b'ha-ya* (syn.). It would seem that if the vowels of the first word are heterogeneous, it should preserve its primitive orthography, retaining the حرف مد *huruf madd* (if any), and in this case it is better not to join the two words. Ex. هارو هار *ha-ru ha-ra* 'tumult, disorder', هارو *ha-ru* 'trouble', and هر *ha-ra* 'disorder', (compare Par. 120), but the words دكچت *duka-chita* 'grief' and سكچت *suka-chita* 'joy' are more correctly written without the و , because as we have seen (Par. 93) the words دك *duka*, and سك *suka*, though usually written with و , should not properly have a

---

* This is the etymology given by FAVRE, but there is a kind of two masted vessel called *ba-lang*, and it seems more probable that the Malays, being essentially a maritime nation, called the commanders of vessels by this term, and in time of war they would be important sectional commanders, whether by sea or land.

long vowel, even when isolated. The modern practice is, however, to assimilate these combined words to the Malay standard, and write دكچيت *dukachi-ta*, and سكچيت *suka-chi-ta*.

136. If the first word has a closed syllable it preserves its primitive orthography, as بارڠسياڤ *ba-rang-siapa* ' whoso-ever'. بليروڠ *ba-lay-ru-wang* ' hall of audience ' (lit. hall of columns), بارڠكالي *ba-rang-ka-li* ' perhaps, very likely ', تدأڤتياد *ta-da-pat-tiya-da* ' necessarily, must ', (an emphatic affirmative formed with two negatives ' but me no buts '). توانهمب *tu-wan-hamba* ' my master ', همبتون *hamba-tu-wan* ' your servant ', ڤرميسوري *p'r-may-su-ri* ' queen '.

137. The words forming a compound may, as we have seen, be joined by submitting to certain changes, but, in most cases, they may remain separate, and, in that case, they preserve their primitive orthography, as in جوربهاس *ju-ru b'ha-sa* ' interpreter, man of languages ' جورباتو *ju-ru ba-tu* ' leadsman, mate ' بلتنترا *ba-la tant'ra* ' army '. A large number of idiomatic combinations of words are found in Malay, but those, not coming within the above descriptions, are mostly written separately, for instance :— چري بري *ch'rray b'rray* ' hither and thither ', چمبوچور *ch'mbu chu-ra* ' toying and chattering ', چمڤڠ چمڤيڠ *chumpang champing* ' torn and ragged ', ڤنتڠ ڤنتيڠ *punting panting* ' headlong sprawling ', لنتڠ توكڠ *lintang pu-kang* ' pell-mell ', تڠڬڠ لڠڬوڠ *tunggang langgong* ' topsy-turvy ', الڠ كڤالڠ *a-lang kapa-lang* ' insignificant ', هين دين *hi-na di-na* ' poor and lowly ', and many others. In addition to these the Malays are very partial

to the use of synonyms, and often borrow a foreign word, and use it in combination with a native word of nearly similar import. In these cases, however, the two words almost invariably remain separate, the following are examples :— مول اصل *mu-la as'l* 'origin, source', عقل بودي *àkal bu-di* 'intelligence, sagacity', أصول فرقس *usūl preksa* 'circumspect', داي اڤاي *da-ya upa-ya* 'device, stratagem, ways and means', لمه لمبت *l'mah l'mbut* 'soft and sweet', تلنجع بواﺕ *t'lanjang bu-lat* 'naked', يتيم ڤياتو *yatīm piya-tu* 'orphan', رندو دندم *r'ndu d'ndam* 'longing', سند گورو *sanda gu-rau* 'jest', كلو كسه *k'lu k'sah* 'sigh', كوﺕ كواس *ku-wat kuwa-sa* 'power, ability', كرام ڤاڤ *k'ra-ma pa-pa* 'poor and lowly', گند گلان *gonda yula-na* 'sad and sorrowful', سوكو كرابت *su-ku k'ra-bat* relatives', ارتي معني *arti màna* 'sense, signification, meaning '.

SECTION XIX.

CONCLUSION.

138. Such are the main principles governing the Malay Orthography, but, as was remarked earlier in these pages, ordinary writing is by no means in strict conformity with them. The departures mainly consist in a much freer use of the weak letters to take the place of the omitted vowel signs, but there is therein absolutely no regularity or established usage upon which a definite rule can be laid down.

139. The most noticeable variations are :—(1) The retention of the weak letter in the penultimate of the radical, after the accent has been changed by the application of a suffixed particle. (2) A general tendency to preserve the orthography of the radical word in the derivatives formed from it. (3) The use of a long vowel in closed syllables on which the accent falls, as اومڤن *umpan* ' bait ', for أَمڤن . (4) The use of ي and و in place of their homogeneous vowels in closed syllables upon which the accent does not fall, if there be a risk of the word being, without some indication of the proper vowel to be applied, mistaken for another word of similar orthography, as امڤون for أَمڤن *ampun* 'pardon', which, in the latter form, might be mistaken for *umpan* ' bait', and توليس for تولس *tu-lis* ' write ' which, in the latter form, might be read *tu-lus* ' sincere '. (5) The marking of all duplications indiscriminately by ٢ . (6) The misuse of ء .

140. Where the derivative words are in as common use as the primitives, they are mostly found written correctly,

because they have been handed down from those, who understood the principles of their formation, but derivatives formed
by the writer are, as often as not, incorrect, from ignorance of
the rules by which their formation is governed. The following passage occurs in the Hikayat A'bdullah, after speaking of
the many old writings and books he studied, and used as his
models, he says :— مک دالم سمڤن‌عن يغ ترسبوة ايتوله اکو ڤراوله
کباڤقکن سمڤون ڤرکتأن دان ايکاتن ڤرکتأن دان رڠکي ڤرکنأن دان
رڠکسکن ڤرکتأن دان لنجوتکن ڤرکتأن *maka da-lam simpan simpa-
nan yang t'r-s'but itu t'h a-ku p'r-o-leh ka-bana-kan simpo-lan
p'r-kata-an dan ika-tan p'r-kata-an dan rangkay p'r-kata-an
dan ringkas-kan p'r-kata-an dan t'njut-kan p'r-kata-an '* from
the stores mentioned, I obtained many connectings of words,
and bindings of words, and unions of words, and abbreviations
of words, and prolongations of words', showing tolerably clearly
that he merely copied derivatives, and did not analyse them.
This short sentence contains at least 7 peculiarities of orthography, not to say of grammar, for which it is difficult to
account. Correctly written it would read :— ملک دالم سمڤن
سمڤنان يغ ترسبت ايتله اکو ڤراوله کبڤاکن سمڤولن ڤرکتاعن دان اکاتن
ڤرکتاعن دان رشکايي ڤرکتاعن دان رڠکاسن ڤرکتاعن دان لنجوتن ڤرکتاعن

141. And so throughout the book frequent variations and
mistakes of spelling occur*. Nothing can possibly excuse the
writing of سهبيا for سهايي *s'ha-y-t* ' servant, slave, (used
as a pronoun of the first person)'. Opening the book

---

* Some of the errors may have arisen on the reproduction of the book.
The edition quoted from is the lithographed one, published under the auspices
of the Straits Branch of the Royal Asiatic Society in 18 0.

casually we find مأكن ممينم دان منوليس *ma-kan mi-nu-n dan m'nu-lis*; here are three words, each properly having the long vowel and accent in the open penultimate, and the ultimate of each a closed syllable, with instances of the three vowels, and for what possible reason should the last alone have a weak letter in the ultimate syllable? Nor is the author consistent in the formation of derivatives, for, in one phrase we find راجن *ra-ja-ña* (for رجان) and لمان *lama-ña*. In one place we find *ka-ada-an* ' existence' written كداّن, and two pages later كد'ٴن instead of كُدّٴن. Take another instance, تيد سمڤت دسمڤيت *tiya-da sumpat di-sumpit.* In this instance, why is the ي inserted in the latter word? Had a و been used in the penultimate and accented syllable, it would not have been difficult to assign a reason, even though an incorrect one.

142. Taking casually the title page of a native pamphlet, we find, تركارغ دان تراتور ددالم سيڠڤورا . Here are 10 weak letters quiescent used in five words, and not more than 4, or at the outside 5, can be justified by the pronunciation, if they are considered letters of prolongation of sound. تركارغ دان تراتر ددالم سيڠڤور *t'r-ka-rang dan t'r-a-tur di da-lam si-ngapu-ra.*

143. The student will however find, that, especially in the older writings, a large proportion of the words are correctly and consistently written, and will find in them authority for the rules of orthography contained in this book, the exceptions mainly tending to show, either a want of knowledge of principle, or a capricious departure therefrom. The phrases

quoted in this work are nearly all transcribed from books, and, beyond correcting the forms of the letters, the orthography has not been changed without showing how the words were spelt in the original.

144. The following is a sample of Malay Orthography literally transcribed, followed by its equivalent in Roman letters, showing where some of the letters seem to have been wrongly applied, and a translation. The same extract is repeated in lithographed manuscript, and a few other specimens of Malay handwriting have been added: —

حتي ببراف لمان انق فومفوان ايتقون بالغله سرة دغن بايك فارسن ملك اقبيل دليهت اوله اورغ برتف اية اكن انقي تله بسربه مك اي بركاة كفد استرين ادفون انقكو اين فاتقله كيت فرسوامين دغن اورغيغ بركواس لاڬي ڬاڬه براني مك اورغ برتف ايتقون ممغٝل راج متهاري مك ايفون داتغله مك كاة اورغ برتف ايت امبلله تونهب اكن انق هامب اين منجادي استري تونهمب مك جوابن بوكنى اكو كواس اون ايتوله منوتف اكو مك ايته بركواس درفد هامب مكدٝغٝلن اون سرة بركاة كهوبنله اغكو دغن انقكو اين مك جواب اون اكو تياد بركواس ملينكن اثين ايتوله بسر كواسن درفد هامب مكدٝغٝلن ٝول اثين مك كاة اثين اكو تياد بركواس ببراف بسر اثين سكاليفون دتاهن اوله سدوه ڬونغ مك دثٝغٝل ٝول راج ڬونغ مك كتني

اكو تيد كواس سميكور تيكرس بونه ٠٥ورق اكو ايله ترنبه بسر
كواسن ٠ك دئكاپله راج تيكوس ٠ك ستله سده ئوتسله بچارا
٠ك راج تيكوس ايتوله هندق كهوين دغن انقن ايت ٠ك
جواب راج تيكوس جكلو استريكو ايت جادي سفرة اكو
بولهله اكو كهوين دغندي ٠ك سكارغ اين اي مانسي اثاك
ئريكو كهوين دغندي

Hatta b'bra-pa lama-ña a-nak p'rampu-wan (ا unnecessary,
Par. 55) *i-tu-pun ba-ligh-lah s'rta* (ت should be employed,
Par. 29) *d'ngan bayk pa-ras-ña maka apabi-la di-li-hat o-leh
o-rang b'r-ta-pa i-tu a-kan a-nak-ña t'lah b'sar-lah mak i i-ya
b'r-ka-ta* (ت) *k ipada istri-ña ada-pun a-nak-ku i-ni pa-tut-
lah ki-ta p'r-suwami-kan d'ngan o-rang-yang b'r-kuwa-sa lag-gi
ga-gah b'ra-ni maka o-rang b'r-ta-pa i-tu-pun m'manggil raja
mataha-ri maka iya-pun da-tang-lah maka ka-ta o-rang b'r-ta-pa
i-tu nmbil-lah tu-wan-hamba a-kan a-nak hamba i-ni m'nja-di
istri tu-wan-hamba maka jawab-ña ba-kan-ña a kn kuwa-sa
a-wan itu-lah m'nu-top a-ku maka i-yalah b'r-kuwa-sa d'ripada hamba maka di-panggil-ña a-wan s'rta b'r-kata ka-win-
lah* (كاوين Persian) *angkaw d'ngan a-nak-ku i-ni mak i jawab
a-wan a-ku tiya-da b'r-kuwa-sa m'layn-kan a-ngin* (ى
unnecessary) *i-tu-lah b'sar kuwasa-ña* (كوسان , Par. 120)
*d'ripada hamba maka di-panggil-ña pu-la a-ngin maka ka-ta
a-ngin a-ku tiya-da b'r-kuwa-sa b'bra-pa b'sar a-ngin s'ka-li-
pun di-ta-han o-leh s'bu-wah gu-nong maka di-panggil pu-la
ra-ja gu-nong maka kata-ña a-ku tiya-da kuwa-sa s'-e-kor*

(و unnecessary, Par. 90) *ti-kus* (و unnecessary, Par. 90)
bu-leh m'ng-o-rek (ى unnecessary, Par. 90) *a-ku iya-lah t'r-l'bih*
kuwa-sa-ñ t maka di-panggil-ña-lah (دثكُلبه , Par. 121) *ra-ja*
ti-kus ma'en s't'lah sudah pu-tus-lah bicha-ra (final ! unnecessary,
Par. 46.) *maka ra-ja ti-kus itu-lah haudak ka-win d'ngan a-nak-*
ña'i-tu maka jawab ra-ja ti-kus jikalaw istri-ka ja-di s'p'rti
(ت) *a-ku bu-leh-lah a-ku ka-win d'ngan-diya maka s'ka-rang*
i-ni i-ya ma-nusiy t apa-kah pri-ku ka-win d'ngan-di-ya.
'Now after a while the girl grew up to be a woman, and also
of goodly appearance, and when the hermit saw his child was
grown up, he said to his wife, ' It were well we married our
child to a person of power, strength and courage ', so the
hermit thereupon called King Sun, who came, and the hermit
said, ' Let My Lord take his servant's child to wife ', but he
replied ' It is not I, who am powerful, but the Clouds, they
can shut me in, and are more powerful than I '. So he
(the hermit) summoned the Clouds, and said, ' Marry my
daughter '. But the Clouds replied, ' It is not we, who are
powerful, but the Wind, its power is greater than ours ', so he
called the Wind also, but the Wind said, ' I am not powerful,
however great the Wind may be, a single Mountain can arrest
it ', so he called King Mountain, who said, ' I have no power, a
single Mouse can rend me, it is he whose power is greatest '.
So he called King Mouse, and when they had taken counsel,
King Mouse was willing to marry the child, but said, ' If she
become even as I am, then could I marry her, but at present
she is human, what would my circumstance be, married to
her ? '

حتى بواوطلان انوقومغوزا ايتغوت بالعقليرة دغنايرم
قلاس ايكل افيل لبهتا ادماورانع بناوادىن اكن انغت تلدبسرلد
مكاي بكاه كفه بمتربت اد افوز انتكهان خاتتلكت زرسوام
كن دختنا اورتيغ بركوسلم لاكن كاكذبرافن كاوانع بناخابغون
منتكلاح متهارا كالعغوز انتلد مكاه اوراني بناوادىه الجبلد توك
مجدكن انوقمرن غاتخايتربب نذاهتجمكجواب بوكن اككهكلاون
البنورلمننو نوكومكالبلد بركوس درغد جمن مكا فقطلخن اوانلمرفدبكاه
كهمونذلدعكو دغزانتكاف مكجوب اوان كونيادبركو مينكن
انغت ابنله بسربركوكلن درغدجمنكد فقطلخن فزلنغزمكاه انغت
اكرنيادبوكوكلم بجراوز بسرابغن ساليغنذ نذاجو ادلسوه كونغ
مكرفقطلخلنفوزاج كونغ مكن كنا اكرنيادا كوكلن بنكورونشكورس بولدمغورمذر
اككبلد توبد بسربركوكان مكرفقطلخلد لاج نكورسن مككنكملد فوسدعار
بكوردج ينكوكو ابىله نو كهونزو ذذنا انوونذن مكرجوب لاج نكوكو لاج
بدرزسغزكوبولجبلدا كوكهونزرعت سمكركارانا يانى لانه فكككغزيكورغكروف

دغندب

أ

مكراونيو برسومين لالوبرجالنزد وابركود ارمكوه هومتن كلواهمومتن
نايتهوكبد نوزبوكيت دان نايت پانونوزياتو دان نزكوليغه دان
ماكن فوزنياو دان نياد مينوم حقي دعالم دمكين ايةكت بركوليغه
مكراهفين لالومنوجومستهارمعهلف دان بيراؤ لمان ابوملالو ومومتن
دان ريايغ بسر مان ملالو بوكيت بنتگكيد دان بيراؤ ابي برتوبغن
بناتغ بغ بولن بكراي برجالن ايةمكبده وكلووار بيراؤ لماء دان
انتاراء ابي برجالن ايةسكبتاد الدجواابرتمووغزبولوه فيهندوابة
بيراؤ لماء دان انتاراء ابي برجالن اية ابي برجالن مكه انغلكفذ سانومارى مكه
نوزنيلمهموجمن دان اعين ريبوة بسة طوفن كالح كابوة كالكه كخميتا
نياد كليهاتن سراة الدمكه ككفمري وغن اندرابغساوان اؤ نوزبروبرؤ
ستله هيلغ موجمن دان اعين ريبوة دان طوفن اية مكه ليهتن
سومارت نياد لكه كليهاتن بتكككفمري فوزبمخاري اندرابغساوان مكه
اندرابغساوان بمخارى كغني اؤكفن نياد جواابرتموه مكيند حالن
انغلح كدوا ابركود دابة دعالم هموتزريبايت.

حكايت اندرابغساوان

مڠهڤون بيغ اورڠ كاﭬغ
بنتغ دلاغت دافة دبـلغ
جلا مجلا اوفة مغووفت
غراوان كاﭬغ لكوت جنداال
بوكين بكي فراوان دهولو
كاﭬغ اين بيده ترلالو
دمان بابق انق تروت
كلكواﭬغ ايت بربابي ورت
كجوالي انف، سكاﭬغ اين
سام برماتن كسان سيفي
كلين ابة تند علامة

علموث بابق فهمن كدﭬغ
تيدق كد موكات هارغ
راجي برسوال ككنف تمفت
دغن تروت فراوان برسمد
بابق منارڠ كوفن دان مالو
بارغ بجارڠ كلين تاه
انف فراوان ادڠ سان
كسدا هنن ايّة بربوغ نزيند
الكلاكي دان فرمفوان كام برابي
سباكي اورغ لاكي بيني
امفين كراغن صاءه قيامة

بهوا اين دوقتة الاخلاصى وتمنة الاجلس سرة كلمه سابغ يغ
ابتيادو برفتوسن دان بركسدهن سلاك اوفراداان چكراوا العهاري دان
بولن بايتة ودخبيت نوئكوطبالدين ابن المرحوم فدو كبسرى سلطان
زين العسيد حليم شاه يغ ممغكو دان مغانور مرنته نهكن كرجاان نكرى قدح
دارالامن بارغ ددهلكن اولدتو هند سركو سكلين علم اغال الجو الكيرات
واننع تنهصاوذن بجلس حمايتة بيت بغترا تام توزبهموبة فريدورق الويبس
ديلىيغ مربنة وذملكس اين تيكي دوه نكرى بايتة سيغانور افول يغع دان
ملاك سرة سكلى جماهن دان دنتو دان ابوهد ديع ساغتة عريف بجتاان كم
منشهو كمعين كمنعكان بمرة ساغتة عليل مروة انتس سكل صحابتث
قريب دان بعيد .

ديعسلد دورفداايت بمرة معلمكن او الممودن
صحابة ستة يغ بتاريخ قده هارو بولن جولي قامر ٤٤٥١ سلد
وصل كنديبت دان سكلين بغترا كبست دالمن تله مغهملديبت اوان .

. . . .

دفريءوة ممدكذاين قدليم ابكبر هاري بولن صفرندة هارو احمد فلد من سله

145. The following is an example of a very correct style. It is an extract from the work known as شجرة ملايو *Shajarat M'la-yu*, and with its orthography little fault can be found. A few suggested corrections are shown in parentheses:—

ستله لقسمان سده برکات ايت لالو مڠمبه ڤد سلطان ابراهيم
تله براڤ هاري دسيك ايت مك لقسمان ڤون برموهن ڤد
سلطان ابراهيم مک سلطان ابراهيم ممبري ڤرسالين [ڤرسالن]
اکن لقسمان هڠ ترە دان ڤرسمبه سورت کملاك دمکين بوڽيڽ
ڤاتك ککند امڤون سمبه داتڠ کڤد ڤادک [ڤدوک] ادند
جکلو اد خيلف ببل ڤادک ککند مليکن امڤون [امڤن]
ڤادک ادند باڽق٢ اکن ڤادک ککند ملك سورت ڤون دارق
اورڠ کڤراهو مک لقسمان ڤون کمبالي کملاک ملك سورت ڤون
دارق برݢاجه ڤايوڠ [ڤايڠ] ساتو کونيڠ [کونڠ] ساتو اوڠو تله
داتڠ کڤننتو لور مک ݢاجه ددرمکن دسان ݢندڠ ڤايوڠ سهوان
تڠݢل دلور سورت جوݢ دباو ماسق کدالم دان سورت ڤون
دباچ اوله خطيب تله سده دباچ سورت ايت مک لقسمان
ڤون منجنجڠ دلي لالو دودق ڤد تمڤتڽ سدي کال ملك سلطان
علاءالدين برتان ڤد لقسمان هڠ توه مک اوله لقسمان سکل ڤري
حالن دسيک ايت سهوان دڤرسمبهکن کباوه دلي سلطان
علاءالدين ملك بݢند ڤون ترلالو سکچيت دان ممبري انݢره اکن
لقسمان دڠن سڤرتيڽ دمکينله استعادة دهولو کال جاڠنکن
ددالم نݢري ملاك ايت داڤت ممبونه دڠن تياد سداهو راج
جکلو تعلق کملاك ڤون تياد بوله ممبونه دڠن تياد برتان

146. The Arabic system of orthography is intended to be strictly phonetic, but is too complex for a language of such simplicity of sound as the Malay, and the attempt to apply it in its entirety has had a result, which is not surprising when one considers the small opportunities for systematic instruction which have generally been available for the bulk of the Malay race. That a modified form of the Arabic system would have sufficed is probable, but no attempt was made to formulate one. The earlier writers evidently attempted to follow the Arabic, and knew, and understood, its peculiarities. As civilization spread, and the necessity for a knowledge of reading and writing became more general, the difficulty of teaching such an elaborate and refined system as the Arabic, more particularly as it was very unsuited to Malay, seems to have soon led to the omission of the vowel signs and orthographical marks, which are integral parts of the Arabic system, though the spelling dependent upon their use, and which, without them, is incomplete, continued to be used, and has resulted in what is little better than a shorthand of consonants. As elementary education becomes more general, however, the knowledge of the system upon which the Malay orthography was based does not appear to keep pace with it, and it may be said that, at the present day, a comparatively small proportion of Malays look upon the rudimentary principles of the Arabic system as part of the Malay orthography. From the slight means of intercommunication, or for the exchange of ideas, and from the tendency of the Malays not to form large communities, and hence the

absence of any recognized seat of native learning, numerous conventions have grown up independently, some of them perhaps depending upon peculiarities of local accent and pronunciation, but more arising from independent attempts to remedy the defects of the existing system of orthography.

147. It is not difficult to understand that a person whose elementary education has not gone much beyond learning the letters of the Alphabet, and who hears them called *ba, ta,* &c., and not having been taught that the vowel is not necessarily part of the letter, will naturally assume that the sound of '*a*' accompanies the letter unless the presence of another vowel be by some means indicated, and so, he will write correctly كمبيڠ *k'mbang* 'to expand, bloom, flower', but will probably insert a و in the first syllable, and write كومبيڠ for كمبيڠ *kumbang* 'the carpenter bee', and a ي in the last syllable, and write كمبيڠ for كمبيڠ *kambing* 'a goat', for how can he know that such words are supposed to be written, كمبيڠ كمبيڠ and كمبيڠ respectively? The tendency to use the weak letters و and ي in place of their homogeneous vowels, to a much greater extent than ا is used in place of its corresponding vowel, may owe its origin to a period of which no authentic record has yet been discovered. In the Korinchi characters, supposed to be those used in Malay before the Arabic Orthography was applied to it, each consonant is (according to MARSDEN) a syllable ending in *a*. The only vowels which have distinguishing marks are *i* and *u*, and there is no sign for eliding the inherent vowel (*a*). That the total omission of vowel

signs from a word, the orthography of which is in other respects correct, produces a very defective representation of the word, will be very apparent from another example :—بِنتَڠ represents equally well *bantang* (the name of the great houses in which the wild inhabitants of Borneo congregate (CRAW-FURD), *b'ntang* (to spread out, or over), *b'nting* (name of a two-masted vessel), *bintang* (a star), *benteng* (battery, rampart), *bentong* (name of a place), or *bunting* (pregnant).

148. It may be said, with little fear of contradiction, that no two native authors spell entirely alike, and that the spelling of no work is consistent throughout, so, all that can be done for the assistance of the student, is to lay before him that which appears, after careful consideration of the various styles, to be the most consistent, and to attempt to formulate the principles upon which it depends.

149. We have said that the system is phonetic and therefore, in the formation of derivatives, the ear should be the safest guide, but the student must bear in mind that the language spoken in the markets and trading settlements, by all sorts of nationalities, is rarely good Malay, and that even the well educated Malays usually assume the dialect, when speaking to Europeans, and further that, as in most Eastern languages, there is a considerable difference between the style adopted in writing, and that used colloquially. In reading it is much more common to adopt a sort of intonation, with little emphasis, but with a more careful articulation and accent than is used in ordinary speech.

150. It will be patent to most students that the orthography

in general use for correspondence, &c., to-day varies
considerably from that employed in the older writings, and it
may be surmised that it is in a state of transition. A large
part of the Arabic system has been neglected, but no definite
modification of that system has been formulated. It may be
that one is in course of evolution, and will be hereafter
defined and regulated by rules. Some indications of the
changes taking place will be found in these pages, but few
have reached the stage of general recognition. The tendency
of the variations may be thus briefly summarized :—

(1.) To employ ﻭ and ﻱ in place of their homogeneous
vowels in closed syllables upon which the accent falls. As
in بلوم *b'lum* 'not yet', سومڤه *sumpah* 'to curse', كريڠ
k'ring 'dry', كچيل *kichil* 'small'. This peculiarity is especially marked in those words in which the penultimate
syllable has the indefinite vowel open, as in :— بتول *b'tul*
'correct', تروس *t'rus* 'through', ڤروت *p'rut* 'belly',
سبوت *s'but* 'mention', تڤوڠ *t'pong* 'flour', رنوڠ *r'nong*
'meditate', لسوڠ *l'song* 'a mortar (for pounding)', تدوه
t'doh 'calm', بنيه *b'nih* 'seed', &c., and it must be admitted
that the words of this class show in their pronunciation the
nearest approach in the Malay language to the sound of long
vowels in closed syllables.

(2.) To similarly employ ﺍ, but only when the first letter
of the syllable is one to which ﺍ cannot be joined (*see* Par.
23), as in كراس *k'ras* 'hard', دان *dan* 'and'.

(3.) To use ﺍ to represent *a* initial in any intermediate
or final syllable, if it follows a letter to which it is not joined,

whether in place of the omitted تشديد *t'shdîd* (*see* Par. 55), in which case the practice would appear to be an improvement, if it were consistently followed, as conveying a better idea of the pronunciation of the words, for example بواه *bu-ah* 'fruit', توان *tu-an* 'master', or in place of همزة *hamzah*, as in هلوان *halu-an* 'prow' for هلوءن . But two *alifs* never occur together in the same word. It would be a great improvement, however, to use ء in all these instances (*see* Pars. 55, 60, 61 and 116).

(4.) To employ و or ي in any closed syllable at the discretion of the writer, in place of the vowel sign, whenever he may consider that it is possible the word may be mistaken, without it, for another, as توليس *tu-lis* 'write' and تولوس *tu-lus* 'sincere'.

151. It follows of necessity that any work, dealing with so indefinite a subject, must be open to a large amount of adverse criticism, but it is hoped that these pages may, at least, direct attention to a very interesting subject, and, in praying for leniency for their faults and imperfections, the reader is asked to remember that no one can be more sensible of their incompleteness than the author.

THE END.

The whole question as to the employment or omission of
ﯘ after the particles ﻣﯩﯔ *m'ng* and ﭙﯩﯔ *p'ng* to denote the
elision of the hard letter, aspirate or آ , as the case may be,
turns upon a very simple issue. Are they to be treated as
closed syllables or not? ROBINSON expressed himself de-
cidedly in the affirmative. If he be right, then, whenever the
syllable following the particle begins with a vowel sound,
whether originally, when this vowel is borne upon آ , or
whether by the deletion of an initial hard letter, or aspirate,
then it follows that a ﯘ must be used, to support the vowel of
which the fulcrum is thus lost. MARSDEN'S Grammar (at page
53) contains the following remark :—" When the primitive
" begins with ﺍ *a* or ﮬ *h* followed by a quiescent letter, or
" what we term a long vowel, those previous letters are
" suppressed, and the particle unites with the long vowel, as
" from ﺍﯨﻜﺖ *ikat* 'to bind' ﻣﯖﯨﻜﺖ *m'ng-ikat,* from ﮬﺎﺑﺲ
" *hăbis* · to finish ', ﻣﯖﺎﺑﺲ *m'ng-abis*; the elision being
" commonly denoted by the orthographical mark *hamzah.*'t
FAVRE quotes this passage in support of the contention that
the vowel of the deleted letter is properly borne upon the ﻉ
ng of the particle, and that no ﯘ is necessary ; he, however,

not quite fairly, concludes his quotation at the words ' long
vowel ', and omits to state that in MARSDEN'S remarks upon
the employment of the mark *hamzah* (at pp. 22 and 23), in
every instance of the particles ‏مڠ‎ *m'ng* and ‏ڤڠ‎ *p'ng*, the
‏ڠ‎ is marked with a ‏جزم‎ *jazm*; ‏ثغداون‎ *peng-adáp-an*
presence, ‏ثغيبر‎ *peng-íbur* comforter, ‏مغوسك‎ *meng-
úsik* ' to tease,' ‏مغمبر‎ *meng-ambur* to scatter, ‏مغونس‎
meng-únus, to unsheath, ‏مغابس‎ *meng-ábis* to consume,
‏مغالو‎ *meng-álau* to drive out . (It is only fair to state that
the Abbé FAVRE does not appear to have quoted from the
original work, but from a translation of it*.) MARSDEN, however, does not, in the remainder of his book, employ the ‏ء‎
when a long *a* follows the particle, as in ‏ثغاسه‎ *p'ng-a-soh*
' nurse ', nor, to the best of our belief, in any single instance to
mark the elision of ‏ك‎ *k* initial. His work must be taken as
one of the highest authority, and bears upon it the stamp of
careful study, and a long and wide examination of Malay writings, and, though he may not have treated this part of the subject with so much careful theory as the Abbé FAVRE, yet his
conclusions are more likely to be in accord with the practice
of the Malays themselves, even if not strictly defensible, and
with them must rest the ultimate decision. Though published
80 years ago, MARSDEN'S work still stands pre-eminent among
English works upon the subject, and remains a lasting
monument to his genius and labour. The translators
of the Bible employ the ‏ء‎ to denote the elision of the

* W. Marsden. Grammaire de la langue malaie, traduite de l'anglais par C. P.J.
Elout.

ك‎ *k* initial, and, after a very careful study of the pronunciation given by the Malays to these derivatives,
we incline to the opinion that when they take the forms مَعْ‎
and ‎ نَعْ‎ they are always closed syllables. FAVRE, however,
makes out a strong case to the contrary, and his work is
one of very careful compilation and great utility, and it is to be
regretted that he should have allowed his attachment to
theory to suggest a doubt as to its authority.* The
strongest point in favour of his view is undoubtedly the repetition of the nasal sound only, in the duplications mentioned
in Par. 132, the initial letter of the particle being omitted in
the repetition. ROBINSON, on the other hand, who went more
deeply into the principles of Malay Orthography, than any
other author, and probably had better opportunities of studying older native writings than are readily available at the
present day, makes the following observation :—" ك‎ takes نَعْ‎
" *pǎng* and ‎ مَعْ‎ *mǎng*, but is itself changed into *hamzah* ; as
" نَعْكَارَغْ‎ *pǎngarang* a composer of a book." So strongly
does he advocate the treatment of these and all the other prefixed particles, consisting of two letters, as closed syllables,
that he appears to insist that, if the particle lose its second

---

* The re-arrangement of the order of the letters of the Alphabet is extremely
useful to the student in explaining certain of the euphonic changes, but the basing
of the whole superstructure of his Dictionary upon this theoretical classification
impairs the utility of the work, and throws considerable difficulty in the way of
those who consult it. The order of the letters of the Arabic Alphabet is well
known, and is accepted by the Malays, as well by every nation employing the
Arabic system of orthography. Any additional letters found to be necessary,
being formed by increasing the number of diacritical points of cognate Arabic
letters, are placed next in order to those letters to which the new letters are affili-
ated, and any one, knowing the Arabic Alphabet, has little difficulty in referring to
a work, the arrangement of the references in which is based upon that order.
It is difficult to avoid the conclusion that FAVRE has committed a grave error
in judgment in making the change.

letter, a closed syllable must nevertheless be formed by
employing a تشديد *t'shdīd* to double the initial of the radical
word. He says:—" It seems proper to observe here, once
" for all, that whenever an abbreviation of the prefix takes
" place, as when فَ *pă* is used for فُن *păn* or فُر *păr*,
" م *mă* for مَن *măn*, بَ *bă* and ت *tă* for بر *băr*
" and تَر *tăr*, the first letter of the primitive takes a
" tashdid, as compensation for the rejection of a letter
" from the prefix." The letter غ , however, cannot take
a *t'shdīd* and the only exceptions to the غ *ng* after فَ *p'* and
م *m'* being succeeded by a vowel sound not borne upon
hamzah would appear to be in the few derivatives formed from
radicals, the initial of which is غ *ng*, and thus, from غاغ
nga-nga is formed فَغاغ *p'nga-nga* ' a gaper ', مَغاغ *m'nga-*
nga 'to gape, yawn'. ROBINSON further says :—" It is a gene-
" ral rule that the prefixes form so many separate syllables,
" and that no letter of a prefix can be joined, in the same
" syllable, with any letter of the primitive word. This remark,
" though it may seem superfluous, is really necessary, in order
" to obviate an error, into which the Malays themselves fre-
" quently fall. For example : a person seeing مغرت, written
" as it stands here, which is the way in which it is commonly
" written by careless or ignorant scribes, and being told that
" it should be pronounced *măngarti* would naturally divide the
" syllables thus : مَغَرت *mă-ngar-ti*, placing the *fut-hah* over
" the غ , and thus combining that and the ر into one syllable ;
" for who should know, unless he had been previously informed,

" that there is an omission of the *hamzah*, over which the *fat-*
" *hah* ought to be placed, and that this word should be written

" مغترت *măng-ar-ti?* "

There seems to have been a doubt, at the time ROBINSON
wrote, as to whether ڤ *p'* in nouns of place was a distinct
particle, or an abbreviation of ڤر *p'r*, and, after stating that he
consulted native authority, he gives the following note
(slightly abbreviated) :—" The person whose opinion was re-
" quested on this point, is reputed to be the best Malay scholar
" in Batavia, and is also said to be a very good Arabic scholar.
" He stated that ڤر *păr* is the proper prefix to nouns of place,
" and that when it is contracted to ڤ *pă* the first letter of the
" primitive ought in strict propriety to have a *tashdid*. It is
" however very true that the *tashdid* is not always audible in
" in pronunciation, and especially when the pronouncing of it
" would produce any harshness. Thus though from جودي
" *judi*, to gamble, is formed ڤجودين *puj-ju-di-yan**, a gambling
" place, by prefixing ڤ *pă*, placing a *tashdid* over the ج
" and affixing ن, yet no native, I believe, ever pronounces it
" as if written with a double ج ; for two ج *s* (*jims*), without

---

* Apparently a printer's error. If *hamzah* be employed in the final syllable, the
correct transliteration would be *paj-judi-an*.

" an intervening vowel, would not only sound very harsh and
" unpleasant to a native ear, but also be very difficult to arti-
" culate. It may be observed, that in many other instances,
" where harshness of sound cannot be an object of dread, the
" *tashdid* is but slightly observed in pronunciation. This
" discrepancy between the spelling and the pronunciation,
" may be partly accounted for from the orthography being
" foreign, which perhaps does not, in every case, perfectly
" accord with the pronunciation. " The above note is quoted
to show the tendency to follow the rules of Arabic orthography
and to indicate how certain of the peculiarities of Malay orthography have arisen, which, unless the presence of the orthograpical marks is supposed, are entirely misleading, and one
is not surprised to find such words as نِيُّر *ñi-yor*, ' cocopalm,' commonly written, by persons unacquainted with the
Arabic rules, نِيور , and it must be admitted that *ñior*
would more nearly convey the pronunciation of this word to
an English reader than *ñi-yor*, but a person acquainted with
the Arabic, and not knowing the Malay word, would probably
read نِيور as *ñi-war*.